# PUTNAM AND PENNYROYAL

### PATRICK JENNINGS

ISBN:
0-439-07965-9

Scheduled Pub. Date:
November 1999

Length:
176 pages

Trim:
$5\frac{1}{2}'' \times 8\frac{1}{4}''$

Retail Price:
$15.95

Illustrations:
21 black and white
drawings

Ages:
8 - 12

Classification:
Middle-Grade
Fiction

LC:
98-54218

Grades: 3 - 7

SCHOLASTIC PRESS
555 Broadway, New York, NY 10012

# Putnam & Pennyroyal

by **Patrick Jennings**
pictures by **Jon J Muth**

Scholastic Press · New York

Library of Congress Cataloging-in-Publication Data
Jennings, Patrick.
Putnam & Pennyroyal / by Patrick Jennings. p.    cm.

Summary: While listening to her uncle as he tells a story about grebes, nine-
year-old Cora Lee realizes that he is revealing something about himself
through the characters he creates.
ISBN 0-439-07965-9 (alk. paper)
[1. Grebes — Fiction.    2. Storytelling — Fiction.    3. Uncles —
Fiction.    4. Birds — Fiction.]    I. Title
PZ7.J4298715Co    1999    [Fic] — 21    98-54218

Printed in the U.S.A.    23
First edition, November 1999
The text type was set in 13.75 point Adobe Garamond
Book design by Dave Caplan

ACKNOWLEDGMENTS:

Thanks to Ruth, Anne,

Sandy Anderson, and,

as always, Alison

For Donald Wetzel,
whom I look up to

# Putnam & Pennyroyal

*It was the end of another year, the last day of* December, and my niece, Cora Lee, was paying me her annual visit. Like every other New Year's Eve day since she was old enough to worm her own hook (at age four), the two of us sat bundled up at sunrise on the banks of Coot Pond, fishing. The pond was winter-morning quiet — quiet except for the coots, of course.

"Chonk, chonk, bweep-bweep, BWAAK!" one of them said from the middle of the pond. It sounded like an old tin bike horn.

"Chonk, bweep-bweep-bweep, BWAAK!" another one replied.

The two of them paddled across the surface, pumping their small black heads like pigeons.

Suddenly, the first one stabbed at the water with its pointed white beak and brought up a gooey strand of green slime.

"CHONK! BWAAK! BWAAK!" it honked crossly, then shook off the strand.

"CHONK! BWAAK! CHONK!" said the second.

"BWAAK! BWAAK! BWAAK!" said a third from across the pond.

"I don't see how we're going to catch anything with *them* around," Cora Lee grumbled. I could see her breath. "They're so noisy."

I explained to her that when it comes to coots, there's not a lot can be done. They have their ways, much as we all do, only more so, and it was probably best just to accept them as part of things, and leave it at that.

"But I haven't had a nibble all morning," Cora Lee said, lifting her hook out of the water. Her bait was gone. "Oh!" she said. "Those blasted coots!"

I said that it probably hadn't been the coots at all, that they hadn't come within ten feet of us all day.

"That's not what I mean and you know it!" Cora Lee said. "Those coots ruin everything!"

Don't you suppose the fish are pretty much used to them by now? I asked.

"Just once," Cora Lee said without listening, "why can't we go fishing where there aren't any coots? Why can't we go to a different pond? Why do we always have to come here?"

She always says this when the fish don't bite. But she knows why. She knows that I live in southern Arizona, and that southern Arizona isn't much like northern Indiana, where she lives. She's used

to ponds and creeks and lakes and rivers. But most of southern Arizona, like most of all of Arizona, is a very dry, thirsty place. Water is precious. Ponds are scarce. (Heck, *puddles* are scarce.) Consequently, I've always felt as lucky as a rabbit with all its feet to have Coot Pond. And although I'd told Cora Lee as much on many occasions in the past, I went ahead and told her again. I've heard it said that children like repetition.

She didn't seem to want to hear about how maybe the fish just weren't very hungry right then, how maybe they'd had a leech feast last night or a big bloodworm breakfast already this morning and so were still in bed, well fed and happy.

"Fish don't have beds!" she said.

I asked her if she'd never heard of a riverbed and where it was exactly that she thought trout slept, but she wasn't in the mood for any of my nonsense, and told me so.

"I'm not in the mood for any of your nonsense, Frank," she said.

Cora Lee is my sister Fran's daughter. (Yes, Frank and Fran. Francis and Francine. Our folks were like that.) So, technically, I'm her uncle: *Uncle* Frank. Still, I'm not one to nitpick. If she feels that skipping the Uncle part is right and good and respectful, well then that's fine by me. I'm aware that children have different ideas about such things these days.

"I'm ready to go," Cora Lee said, and jerked in her line. She wound it round her cane pole with a few flicks of her wrist, then she pulled off her fishing hat — the one with the lures and flies that she and I had made sewn to the hatband. Her brown, braided pigtails spilled out and hung suspended behind her ears. She stood up and dusted off the bottom of her overalls. "You coming?" she said exactly as if she were a grown-up.

I told her okay, I suppose I was, but that I sorely wished we could stay just a little while longer on account of this feeling I was having in my right ankle. (That's where I usually get my feelings.)

"You have a feeling in your *ankle?*" Cora Lee said in a hushed tone.

It's rattlin' like a diamondback's tail, I told her in my best old-west, old-timey voice. I left the "g" off "rattling" for authenticity. She likes the old, weathered cowpoke act. Doesn't seem to faze her much that I'm from Indiana, same as she, or that I'm only thirty-three years old. To someone who is nine and seven-twelfths, thirty-three might as well be thirty-three thousand.

It's rumblin' like monsoon thunder, I threw in for good measure.

She put her hat back on.

"What do you think it is?" she asked.

I shrugged. Better, I thought, to let her imagination run.

"Carp?" she said, sitting back down on the bank.

Shrug.

"Bullhead?" she said, worming her hook.

Shrug.

*"Largemouth?"* she whispered, wide-eyed.

Hesitant shrug. I looked at her with what I hoped was a meaningful expression. The expression I was after was something like: Well, I don't want to jinx it, but it surely does feel a whole lot like largemouth to me.

She cast her line.

"How's your ankle?" she said.

Gruntin' like a javelina in the creosote, I said.

"Hot diggedy!" she whooped, and slapped her knee.

I reminded her that noise scared away the fish.

"Right," she said. Her smile disappeared. Her hazel eyes — like my mother's, like Fran's — locked on the tip of her cane pole. Her grip and her mouth tightened. Her knuckles and lips turned white. Her eyebrows met in a line above her nose. (She gets those eyebrows from her dad, Howard. Howard looks as if he has two trained tent caterpillars sleeping above his eyes.)

She sat still as a kingfisher on a low, overhanging branch, waiting and watching for a nibble. Ten minutes went by without her so much as moving a muscle. So I asked her if she'd like a story.

"A fish story?" she whispered.

I said I believed I had used up all my fish stories. I'd told that poor child every whopper I knew, and a few more besides. How about a bird story? I asked.

On cue, a coot honked from the middle of the pond. "Chonk, chonk, bweep-bweep, BWAAK!" it said.

"No bird stories," Cora Lee hissed.

Then how about a grebe story? I suggested.

She wrinkled her nose. "A *what* story?" she said.

A grebe story.

"What's a grebe?"

You never heard of a grebe?

She shook her head. "What is it?"

Well, I said, it's sort of like a bird and sort of like a fish.

She eyed me suspiciously. "More like a bird or more like a fish?" she asked.

This required consideration. I knew she did not want a bird story — she'd made that plain — and I also knew, unfortunately, that a grebe is, zoologically speaking at least, a bird, and that there is nothing so much like a bird as a bird. But I asked myself: Is a grebe really *like* a bird? No! was the answer I emphatically gave. If anything, it is much more like a fish! In fact, there is no bird, the loon included, that is more like a fish than a grebe. Cora Lee herself had never seen or even heard of grebes — this despite the fact that there is almost always one living on Coot Pond — and *why?* Because they are almost always underwater, that's why. Like fish.

And so it seemed to me completely within my right to say to her, Oh, it's much more like a fish! Yet something stopped me. My conscience, I suppose. Just because I am a fisherman doesn't mean that I don't have respect for the truth. I do. It's just that sometimes I don't have much use for it, that's all. But that said, let me add in my defense that I am most commitedly a firm believer in the importance of speaking the truth to children as far as one can really know it, and when it is impossible to get around it.

"Well?" Cora Lee asked. "Which is it?"

I swallowed hard. It's a bird, I said, then quickly added, but it's more like a fish.

Cora Lee squinted at me. "What does *that* mean?"

W-well, I said, feeling the heat of her squint. Well, you see, a grebe is nearly always underwater. In fact, the pied-billed grebe — which is the kind of grebe my story is about — is underwater so much and is such a fine swimmer and expert diver that, in one book I read, a very learned gentleman and naturalist by the name of Leonard Lee Rue III called it a "fish with feathers."

I was trying to get on her good side. Cora Lee is very fond of being in or near water. She is not only a fine swimmer and diver, but also a proficient wader, dipper, and splasher. Said plainly: She's more fish than kid. Still, her expression hadn't changed an iota. The squint was still there.

Some folks, I went on hopefully, have taken to calling pied-billed grebes 'devil divers.'

Her squint only tightened. I was losing her.

Others, I said somewhat desperately, call them 'water witches.'

Her feet wiggled slightly. A good sign. Wiggly feet are a good sign.

Actually, the truth is, *most* people call them "water witches," I said.

Her squint loosened the slightest bit. You had to really be looking in order to see it. Then she said, in a rather leery way, "Okaaaaay."

Okay? I said.

"Okay," she said. "I'll hear the grebe story."

*I only had one grebe story (there may only be* one grebe story): the tale of Putnam and Pennyroyal. Funny that grebes don't have more stories told about them. Other birds certainly have their share. Stories about hens and roosters must run in the hundreds. I myself know a gaggle of goose stories, a paddling of duck stories, and a host of sparrows'. I also know or have heard stories about swans, swallows, nightingales, crows, robins, meadowlarks, gulls, penguins, and owls — I even know a few emu stories. (I'll have to remember to tell them to Cora Lee sometime. They're doozies.)

But just the one grebe story. One would think, considering the peculiar nature of the grebe and the fact that they can be found just about any-where in North America one might choose to look (providing one chooses to look), and that they are just about the closest kin to the archaeopteryx still alive and laying (eggs, I mean), well, one would think folks would show more interest.

Still, that's the way it is, grebewise, and there's no sense in wishing it were otherwise. (I've never been one to put much stock in wishing things were otherwise.) I was grateful to have at least one grebe story, and set myself down to the business of relating it to my one niece — whom I was also very grateful to have.

This is the story of Putnam and Pennyroyal, I said. Putnam was a pied-billed grebe and he lived right here on Coot Pond.

"This is a *true* story?" Cora Lee asked.

Of course, I said. I told her that all my stories were true, that I didn't even know how to make up stories. (This kind of thing is considered kosher so long as one has a fishing license. Which I do. It doesn't expire for another month.)

"There are grebes on this pond?" Cora Lee whispered, looking about. "Where?"

Well, as I mentioned, pied-billed grebes are usually down diving, and there's usually only one on any given body of water, which dims your chances of seeing them. On top of that, they're very shy birds — so shy, in fact, that they eat their own feathers.

"They eat their *feathers?*" Cora Lee said, scrunching up her face. "Why?"

No one's really sure, I said.  They're the only birds that do it. Maybe it's a nervous tic — like biting one's nails.

"You bite your nails," Cora Lee said. "And you're kind of shy. Mama is always saying that you should get out more."

I get out, I said.

"She says you're always fishing," Cora Lee went on. "She says she never hears from you unless she calls."

Do you want to hear this or not? I said.

Cora Lee shrugged her shoulders. "Go ahead,"

she said, then added under her breath, "Nail-biter."

Well, like I said, a grebe is very shy, and its eyes and ears are very sharp — so sharp, in fact, that they're underwater before anything can get within yards of them. Legend has it that at the sight of a gun flash they can dive before the bullet reaches them. But that's a hunter's legend. Hunters aren't very reliable.

"What do they look like?" Cora Lee asked.

Well, they usually wear silly hats with furry flaps that go down over their ears and big coats and hip boots and they almost always carry a gun big enough to knock over an elephant that they use to shoot quail with. But you know. Your dad's one.

"Not *hunters!*" Cora Lee groused. "*Grebes!*"

Oh, I said. Well, there's a lot of different kinds of grebes. Some of them have red eyes and some of them have golden ones, though most of them have black, and one kind, the eared grebe, has ears, though they're not *really* ears, they're just fancy feathers on the sides of their heads. Birds' ears are hidden, you know.

Cora Lee glared at me. "What about *pied-billed* grebes?" she said.

*Pied-billed* grebes? I said, ingenuously. Why, they have black eyes.

"Frank!" Cora Lee barked. "I mean, what do they *look* like? Are they like ducks?"

Well, I said, I suppose they're sort of ducklike. Maybe more loonlike. At least the other grebes are. The pied-billed looks a bit like a chicken. It's sort of chickenlike and ducklike and loonlike all mixed together. They even look a little cootlike, I said, then wished I hadn't. I hurried on before she could fuss.

The pied-billed is one of the smaller grebes, though not the smallest. Its plumage is brownish and furry-looking — kind of like a beaver's coat. The other grebes have long, pointy bills, like loons and coots. (Coots again!) But the pied-billed's bill is like a chicken's, except that, most of the time at least, it has a single black stripe wrapped around it. It sort of looks like its mouth is tied shut.

"Is that what 'pied' means?" Cora Lee asked. "Tied shut?"

I didn't know and I didn't have my bird guide with me at the moment. Or my dictionary. All I could think of was the pied piper. Was he pied? Or was his pipe? How does one "pie" something anyway? I decided to bluff.

"Yes," I said, "but I think it also means striped. Black-and-white striped, I'm pretty sure. Like a magpie. You know: magpied."

Cora Lee looked at me with a confused expression. I changed the subject.

One of the reasons grebes swim and dive so well, I said, is that they have lobed toes. They're not bony like a chicken's or webbed like a duck's. They're sort of in between. They look a lot like lizard toes, actually, only more flappy. Think of earlobes and you'll be on the right track. Grebes are the only diving birds that have lobed toes. The only other kinds of birds that have them are wading birds, like the snipe and the sandpiper, and the — I almost said it again. The C word. I peeked at my niece out of the corner of my eye to see if she'd noticed. She'd noticed.

"The what?" Cora Lee asked, scowling at me. "The *coots?*"

As if on cue, the coots on the pond honked.

Cora Lee turned her scowl on them.

Of course, I hastened to add, pied-billed grebes are much, much, much different than coots. *Much* different. For example, pied-billed grebes are quiet. Coots aren't. Pied-bills pretty much keep to themselves. Coots don't. Pied-bills dive. Coots dabble. Sometimes a coot will dive, but it would never go very deep. Aside from the loon, no bird can dive as fast or as deep or stay down as long as the grebe.

"How about the penguin?" Cora Lee asked. "My teacher said that penguins can dive eight hundred feet."

This was not the first time that Cora Lee's schooling had tried to horn in on one of my stories. It used to be that Cora Lee would listen rapturously to every tale I told her and believe them all without question. Then she started school.

Well, I said to her in a voice that hinted that I was more than just a little bit insulted by her cheek, the grebe can dive deeper than any *flying* bird — with the exception of the loon, naturally. Penguins are flightless, as I'm sure you and your teacher are aware. It only stands to reason that their diving would improve, what with so much time on their hands.

"So grebes *do* fly?" Cora Lee asked with a smirk.

She's such a clever child. She was trying to get out of me that grebes were more birdlike than I was letting on. But I was a step ahead of her.

Only when absolutely necessary, I said. They're not really built for it, you see. Their wings are too small and their feet are too far back. A grebe walking is one of the silliest things you could ever hope to see. And, seeing as how they usually stay on one body of water all year round, year after year, and are much better off diving from danger than flying from it, it is hardly ever absolutely necessary. They really are more fish than bird, I added, then returned her smirk.

"But they have to fly sometimes," Cora Lee said. "If they don't mate, they'll become extinct."

A very clever child. I told her so.

She grinned, then lobbed me another question. "Didn't you say this was the story of Putnam *and* Pennyroyal? What about Pennyroyal?"

You'll find out about her later, I said.

"Is she a pied-billed grebe? Did she live on Coot Pond?"

Later, I said again.

"Well, at least tell me *what* she is," Cora Lee said, irritated. "She's a grebe, isn't she?"

You'll see, Cora Lee, I said — which I so like to say. She's not so fond of it.

"My name is *Cora!*" she snapped. "*Just* Cora!" She raised her hook out of the water. It was bare. "Dumb coots!" she said.

She jerked in her pole, hand over hand, and rewormed her hook, grumbling the whole time. Then she recast her line, flashing me a face that

seemed to say, Say one word to me and just see what happens!

I decided to let a little time roll by. Before too long, her scowl softened and she started drifting off across the water. It's easy to do at the pond — drift off. I leaned back on my elbow and listened to the wind humming and whistling and watched it bend the dried bulrushes and, sometimes, crack them in half. I listened to thrashers sifting through the fallen leaves behind us, sounding like animals much larger and more ferocious than themselves.

The coots, for once, were silent, floating like big black beetles out on the middle, their tiny heads tucked into their wings. Cora Lee sat gazing up at the bare tops of the cottonwoods and willows. Reflected back onto the water, the branches looked like roots.

Without meaning to — which is almost always how it happens — we had settled into a story disposition. So I began again.

*Putnam was brought into this world in the* spring, one of a clutch of six. He was the last to hatch. Like the other chicks, his down was black-and-white striped, like a little zebra grebe. Between his eyes and his bill and at the back of his head were dabs of bright red.

As he was squeezing himself out from his shell, he caught a glimpse of the lobed feet of his mother as she was diving into the pond. The first five chicks were clinging to her feathers and went under with her. Putnam toddled on his new legs to the edge of the floating nest, and, without really giving it much thought, flung himself into the water after them. This was a mistake. Grebes are watertight, of course, but not until their wings have dried. A just-hatched grebe chick's feathers are wet for a few hours at least, which doesn't matter so much when you're clinging to your mother's back, as his siblings were, but it means a lot when you're going it alone.

Putnam sank like a stone. He flapped his tiny, heavy wings in vain as he plunged down into the dark, icy water, down through winding water weeds, down to where the water turned even darker and icier, down to the bottom. He settled at last into the soft, heavy mud of the pond's floor. He flailed and floundered but managed only to dig himself in deeper. Then, exhausted, he lay still on his back, gazing up through the murky water at the duckweed and the frog's-bit and the fluttering golden circle floating on the surface high above.

"The sun," Cora Lee said softly to herself.

After a time, Putnam's eyes began to adjust and he began to see that what he had thought was a deep, black void was, in fact, a pool festooned with life and color. Steely black diving beetles sprung at water fleas, crunching them in their monstrous jaws. Leeches and flatworms drifted past like ribbons. Back swimmers paddled by. A school of mosquito fish appeared and gathered the beetles, the back swimmers, the leeches, and the flatworms into their gaping mouths. Finally, a waxy green bullfrog sprang onto the scene, gobbled up as many of the mosquito fish as it could catch, then sprang out of sight.

Beside Putnam, bloodworms were sprouting up from the mud and waving in the current, turning the water red. They looked as if they were growing from the soil. Instinctively, Putnam rose up as high out of the mud as he could and struck at one of them with his bill, snipping it in half. The bottom half — and the other worms — shrank back into the mud. The top half floated up, out of Putnam's reach.

And then suddenly, from above, a large black form swooped down and scooped up the severed bloodworm in its bill. There were five grebe chicks clinging to its back. Then it was gone.

"Mama?" Cora Lee asked.

It was her all right.

Putnam peered over at the bloodworm patch.

The worm fingers were back out, waving and turning the water red. One was now shorter than the rest. Putnam struck quickly, snipping another finger in half. Again the worms retracted. Again a severed half drifted upward. Putnam gathered what little strength he could muster. His air was running out. He knew somehow that this would be his last chance.

A moment later, Mama returned. As she swooped past, scooping up the bloodworm half, Putnam pushed off the muddy pond bottom with all his might. He rose up high enough to chomp down on her undertail feathers. The jerk almost pulled his head off. But he kept his bill clamped tight, holding on for dear life, until finally he and the rest of the brood were carried up out of the water and safely deposited onto the nest.

Mama regurgitated the food she'd gathered — including the bit of bloodworm Putnam had snipped off for her — into the waiting mouths of her chicks. They clamored and peeped and gobbled up the half-digested food.

Then with a "kuck-kuck-kuck, cow-cow-cow!"

Mama dove back into the water, never knowing how many chicks she had, never seeming much to care. She certainly never counted. It was the chick's responsibility, it seemed, to climb aboard in a timely fashion, or miss the boat, and face the consequences.

The experience left poor Putnam both badly shaken and thoroughly convinced that the depths of the pond were an entirely unwholesome place to visit. From then on, when Mama summoned the chicks with her "mm-put-put-put-put-put-put" call, and the brood gathered on her back for a dive, Putnam just slunk away and curled back into his eggshell. He had hidden it in a twining of rushes before Mama could kick it off the nest into the pond, as she had the others'. Eggshells attract predators, you know.

Cora Lee nodded. "Like hawks," she said, "and eagles."

Putnam understood well the purpose of their missions: they were gathering food. What puzzled him was why the chicks were invited along at all. He couldn't see how they would be of any use with their bills clamped to their mother's feathers. They couldn't catch anything. How could they contribute? What help could they be? He thought and thought about this until one fateful day — as they often say in stories — he learned the answer.

The sky was murky and gray that day. Mama and the brood had gone down hunting quite awhile before. It seemed to Putnam they had been under much longer than usual. Thunder rumbled and bolts of lightning crackled over the cottonwoods and willows. The rushes rustled and whistled. The bullfrogs croaked, "Jug-a-rum, jug-a-rum." The red-winged blackbirds called, "Conquer-RRREEE!" The coots were particularly squawky as they scooted back and forth across the pond, pumping their heads and chonking. Ravens ruffled their waxen wings and clucked their tongues loudly in the cottonwoods overhead. It sounded like coconuts being knocked together. High above, a lone hawk turned lazy, graceful circles. Putnam shivered in his shell, both from the cold and from a chilling feeling he had that something awful was about to happen. He ate a mouthful of down to calm himself, but it didn't help.

"Rock!" one of the ravens above said.

"Rock! Rock! Rock!" the others answered.

Putnam peered up at the enormous black birds, their beaks long and hard and sharp, their eyes cold as night. A shiver ran down his spine. That was it. He had waited long enough. He crept out of his shell and waddled out clear to the edge of his nest. The water was a mirror of the sky: gray and murky and spooky. An icy breeze blew across the pond, rippling its surface and seeping deep into Putnam's tiny bones.

"Mama!" he chirped without really meaning to. "Mama!"

Suddenly, the wind died and the ravens ceased their clucking and the blackbirds their conquer-rreeeing and the frogs their jug-a-rumming, and in the silence Putnam noticed a new sound — low and rumbly, like distant thunder. Quickly it grew to a thrumming, then to a beating — like the beating of his own heart. It was punctured by a

high, shrill SHRAAK! and in the pond Putnam
saw the reflection of a dark, swooping bird.

"Mama?" he peeped as he turned to look. But
instead of his mother he saw a gleaming black eye
and a glimmer of blazing talon — the hawk! —
and suddenly, he was tumbling over, off the nest's
edge, and back into the water.

*I peeked over at Cora Lee. Her mouth was open.*
She was staring up at the sky, watching a hawk cir-
cling high above. Her head circled as she watched.
I let things sink in for a moment, then went on:

This time down, his feathers fully dried, Putnam
found he could swim. In fact, he found he could
swim pretty well. He swam in circles. He swam in
figure eights. Grebes like swimming in figure
eights. He dove down to the bottom. He bit off a
few bloodworms and swallowed them. Delicious!
He swam every inch of the pond, peeked into
every nook and cranny. And he laughed to himself
at the hawk, trapped up in the air, and he laughed
at the ravens in their tree, because he was safe and

free and fast and nothing on earth would ever bring him out of the water again.

Then he ran out of breath.

He resurfaced quietly into a clump of rushes, inch by inch, like a submarine.

"Huh?" Cora Lee said, her brow wrinkled. "What does *that* mean?"

I explained to her how grebes can raise or lower themselves out of the water, bit by bit, how they can stop at any time during the process and remain, for instance, with just their head and neck above water, like a periscope.

She liked that. Her feet wiggled.

And so (I went on) for the first time in his fledging life, Putnam felt happy. He loved diving and he loved swimming. He loved hunting. He soon could catch just about anything he had a taste for. Nothing could outswim him — not mosquito fish or tadpoles or froglets or beetles or leeches or caddis nymphs. He loved the caddis nymphs. They were sweet and crunchy. He loved the froglets and the leeches and the back swimmers. Best of all, though, he loved the bloodworms. They always reminded him of his first meal. He did not, however, love the mosquito fish. They were bitter. After tasting one, he vowed never to eat another.

Time passed, as it often does, and Putnam grew, as the young will. He lost his dabs of red and most of his zebra stripes. Only the stripes on his head and neck remained. He was turning brown. Molting, it's called: one set of feathers comes out, another comes in. Just like a rattler losin' its skin, I said with a slight twang in my voice.

Putnam saw his mother and the brood more and more infrequently as he spent more and more of his time pursuing his newfound aquatic interests. Then, one by one, without Putnam knowing it, his family flew away to find ponds of their own. Mama was the last to leave. I guess in some way she was leaving Coot Pond to Putnam. On the day she flew off — a bright, hot summer day — Putnam was so absorbed in his underwater world that he didn't even notice. Several weeks later it occurred to him that he hadn't bumped into any of them in quite some time, and wasn't that odd? If they *had* flown away — and not been gobbled up by hawks — he felt sure that his mother probably hadn't even looked for him, or even noticed he was missing. She never counted.

After a few more weeks had passed, Putnam had almost forgotten they had ever been existed. He didn't need anyone. He was comfortably fed, comfortably out of predators' reach, comfortably alone down in his watery home. It was almost perfect.

If only it weren't for the coots.

"The coots?" Cora Lee asked, looking up at me.

Oh, Putnam *hated* the coots, I said. *Loathed* them.

"Because they're so noisy, I bet," Cora Lee said. Well, yes, there's that. They're noisy birds, no question about it. And you think they're noisy

now, you ought to hear them when they get it into their heads to fly! Oh, they kick up the biggest fuss you ever heard! You see, coots don't spring up off the water the way ducks do. Coots beat their wings and skitter across the water, kicking at it and pounding at it with their wings, all the while clucking and honking like the end of the world has come. Eventually they manage to lift off, and then, for a brief, blissful interlude, they leave the pond, only to return after barely any time has passed at all. It's hard to say why they even bother.

But at least they do leave sometimes, even if just for a short spell, because when they're here all they do is loiter in the middle of the pond, chattering away about this and that and nothing of any real importance. Putnam could hear them even when he was underwater. If he were ever to surface anywhere near them — which he never meant to do — they would fly at him with their awful chonk-chonk-chonking and their bwaak-bwaak-bwaaking, or they'd break into one of their long-winded accounts of their various adventures and dubious accomplishments. (Coots are notorious for their dubious accomplishments.) If by chance, Putnam had a caddis nymph in his beak, well, they would just snatch it away from him as if it were their birthright to do so. They had no morals whatsoever. They were thieves, plain and simple.

A low hiss escaped Cora Lee's lips.

But for Putnam, the icing on the cake, the last nail in the coffin, the straw that broke the water witch's back, was that those blasted, boorish, babbling birds *adored bloodworms!* As dabblers, of course, they were supposed to confine themselves to the top of the pond. But, for a reason Putnam never understood, these nasty, noisy, pernicious creatures developed a liking for bloodworms and began diving — quite against their nature — down to the pond's bottom to graze. They were soon on their way to ridding the whole pond of the juicy little wrigglers. Clearly something had to be done. They had to be stopped. They were ruining everything. They had to go!

But as Putnam could think of absolutely no way of making them go — he certainly wasn't going to *talk* to them; there's no use *talking* to coots — they remained. Putnam continued to suffer their mind-numbing dialogues, their cackling and honking, their chonking and bwaaking, each day and on into the night, first one story then another and it didn't much matter if they'd told it ten times before, or a hundred, or if the new versions were any different from the previous ones. On and on they prattled and chortled. On and on they plundered and strutted. On and on they ate and they ate and they ate. Until one day, when Putnam had spent the entire morning scouring the pond bottom for breakfast with a particularly acute craving for bloodworms and could find none — not one single wriggler — he said to himself, *That tears it! I'm leaving!*

*There were a couple of things hampering* Putnam's escape. One was that it meant leaving, and, when considered without the coots, Putnam loved Coot Pond. Another was that he had no idea where to go. He had never been anywhere else. And then, of course, there was the simple fact that going meant flying, which was something he had never attempted before. He wasn't even sure he could do it. He had wings — though they were very small wings — and he had a pretty good idea how to use them. He had seen plenty of birds flying over the pond: blackbirds and kingbirds, ravens and vultures, flickers and warblers, towhees and phoebes, woodpeckers, gnatcatchers, sapsuckers, wrens, grackles, grosbeaks, titmice, cowbirds.

Once he'd even seen a groove-billed ani, and another time —

"Frank," Cora Lee interrupted, her palm held up as if to say, That's quite enough.

Sorry, I said. Where was I?

"Putnam had seen lots of birds fly."

Oh, right, right. He'd seen lots of birds fly, and, after all, he thought, even *coots* could do it. How hard could it be? Yet still he had his qualms. (Pied-billed grebes are notorious for their qualms.) He could easily imagine a hundred ways that flying might lead him to a tragic end. There was falling, of course — just dropping from the sky. What if there were essential flight techniques he didn't know about, little tricks of the trade that would prevent him from losing control? A mistake while airborne wouldn't be like a mistake underwater. He wouldn't just float to the surface; he would crash to the ground. And even if he could somehow manage to stay aloft, there would be so many obstacles to dodge — perfect examples being the cottonwoods and willows. And then, of course, there was the matter of other birds, some of which might be hawks or some other variety of grebe-killer.

*No, no, no!* he thought. *It's far too dicey. Far too dangerous. Suicidal, even.* He had to think of something else. *Maybe coots migrate,* he thought.

"They don't, do they?" Cora Lee asked.

I shook my head. They're always here, I said. Why do you think they call it Coot Pond?

"Figures," Cora Lee grumbled.

After deciding that flight was completely out of the question, Putnam rose up from the bottom of the pond — where he did all his best thinking and where all the bloodworms used to be — and surfaced to find one coot telling another coot for the two hundred and fiftieth time how once he had met a loon who had flown into a fog bank and crashed into a mountain, and right then and there, Putnam took off.

To his disappointment, he did not spring up off the pond like a duck. He skittered across the surface, like a coot. He beat at it with his wings and kicked at it with his feet. He even found him-

41

self calling out, "Kuck-kuck-kuck, COW-COW-COW!" He was sure he was making quite a spectacle of himself and was none too pleased about it, when ten feet or so later, he lifted off. Water peeled off his feathers. (The expression could just as easily be, "Like water off a grebe's back.")

The coots were sitting out in the middle of the pond, watching.

"Well, I'll be," one of them said. "It's the grebe!"

"Never noticed it doing *that* before," another said.

"I didn't think it had the nerve," said a third.

"Good riddance, coots!" Putnam called down

as he flew over. "Catch your own meals from now on!"

And with that, he soared up over the rushes and cleared the cottonwoods.

"Rock! Rock! Rock!" the ravens said as he passed over them. Their beaks looked even steelier and crueler up close.

Putnam dropped his feet and raised his bill and quickly climbed twenty feet higher into the air. He looked down to see that the pond had become a small, blue-green oval. The coots were just tiny black dots in the middle, and the ravens, slightly bigger dots in the golden canopy of cottonwood leaves.

Putnam flew on over a crescent of cottonwoods standing alone in a field. The trees were lined up as if they ran alongside a meandering stream, but they bordered only a field of wild grass.

"The oxbow," Cora Lee said. "That's where we always see the great horned owl."

Exactly, I said. But that's mostly because you always visit in winter, when the trees are bare. It's harder to see the old bird when the trees are leafed out.

"I know, Frank," Cora said with one tent caterpillar eyebrow raised. "You tell me that every year."

I hadn't realized.

As Putnam flew over the oxbow, a wave of turkey vultures rose up out of the trees on thermals, their sprawling wings outstretched — six feet from tip to tip — their grizzled red heads looking as if they had been skinned. Putnam did not like the look on their faces. They had the same look Grandpa has when Grandma brings in the Thanksgiving turkey.

Cora smiled. "Grandpa can sure put it away!" she said.

Putnam kicked into high gear. He beat his wings as hard as he could and turned a sudden, fancy about-face. When he looked back, the vultures were far behind him.

*Ha!* he laughed to himself. *I guess I showed them!* In his excitement, he turned a quick, midair figure eight, and then felt a little sick to his stomach.

He was now already far away from the pond. A vast, open landscape spread out below him. He could see no bulrushes or cottonwoods or willows, just small, gnarly bushes and drab patches of dried grass. It was not very inviting. In the distance to his left, he saw a range of craggy brown mountains capped with snow, and to his right, a shorter, snowless range. Ahead of and behind him were two more ranges. Coot Pond was in a basin — a wide, arid river basin that dwarfed his pond to the size of a nickel.

Running alongside the pond, far to his right, was a row of golden-leafed cottonwood trees that extended to the north and south as far as he could see. It looked like some great slithering, gilded serpent. Through the canopy of trees, Putnam saw glimpses of a very lonely little river that ran bravely between the Sonoran and Chihuahuan Deserts.

"The San Pedro," Cora Lee said.

That's the one, I said.

"Why is it lonely?"

Because there aren't many rivers like it flowing in Arizona these days, I said. Most of them are dry nearly all the time, or else they've dried up for good."

"What happened to them?"

Folks, I said, and rocked my hat back on my head. (Her question made me feel wistful and I always rock my hat back when I feel that way. I guess that's because one tends to look up at the sky when wistful.) Folks from other parts of the world (I went on) where there's lots of water. Folks who don't understand the desert, how fragile it is, how important a river here is, even if it's only the size of one of their creeks back home. Folks who like to fish and who like to fish for what they like to fish for. Folks who brought carp and bullhead and largemouth here where they don't belong, not thinking that they might gobble up all the local fish — which is exactly what they did. Folks who trapped the beaver until there weren't any left, and without the beavers, there were no beaver dams, and without the dams, the rivers became fast and low instead of slow and swampy, which is how rivers prefer to be. Folks who brought cattle — lots and lots of cattle — because they had cattle back where they came from and they liked cattle, lots and lots of cattle. And those cows ate everything in sight. It was folks, too, that brought the mosquito fish because they didn't like mosquitoes. They didn't even notice that there was already a fish here that did the job just fine — the Gila top-minnow, quite a capable mosquito fish, and, un-like those exotic ones, not such little pigs. The exotics ate anything they could get into their mouths, including the Gila topminnow.

It was folks that changed the rivers here. And it was folks that dried some of them up, even if they didn't really mean to. It was folks like me, I guess. I rocked my hat back forward over my eyes. (My wistfulness had passed.)

"Will the San Pedro dry up?" Cora Lee asked.

It might, I said. Cows are forbidden here now. Though I still see some from time to time. And the sacaton, the native grass, is starting to come back — a little at least. And they're bringing the beaver back, a few at a time — reintroducing them to their natural habitat. I suppose things are better than they were. It's just that sometimes, when you lose things, you can't ever get them back. Like the passenger pigeon. Or the Monkey

Springs pupfish. They're gone for good. And, you know, if you have a house and you take out too many bricks, you just never know —

"Yeah, yeah — it might pile in on top of me," Cora Lee said, finishing what I had mistaken for an original thought. Then she said, "Maybe we can catch all the fish that don't belong here."

I smiled. We can try, I said.

I checked my line — nothing — and picked up my story:

Putnam climbed higher and higher. It had never occurred to him that there might be so much beyond the pond. He could see for miles in every direction. There was enough room below for thousands of ponds the size of his, but he couldn't find a one. He flew in circles trying to decide which way to go, but finally just decided to follow the river, thinking that, since it contained water and a pond contained water, and there was precious little of it anywhere else, and as the river ran directly by his own pond, well, then maybe it would lead him to another one. And that was what he wanted: a new pond. A pond with blood-worms and caddis nymphs and back swimmers and rushes, and absolutely no coots whatsoever. Not even a little one. He flew northward along the river and kept his eyes peeled.

Putnam found flying to be much more strenuous than swimming, but, on the whole, not all that different. He felt a constant pull downward — whereas in the water the pull was always upward — and he strained new muscles keeping himself aloft. He could dive and climb if he chose to, and he could turn by adjusting the angle of his wings, just as he did underwater. There were dif-

ferences, of course. He never had to surface for air, though he knew he would have to land and rest before too long — his wings were already tiring. There were no rushes to hide in. There was nothing to hide in. There weren't even any clouds. And, then, of course, there was no food: no caddis nymphs, no leeches, no back swimmers. No bloodworms. There were flying insects to be had — flies and bugs and butterflies and such — which he saw other birds catching. One little bright-red bird, in fact, seemed able to turn in any direction, no matter how fast he was flying, in pursuit of a bug.

"A vermilion flycatcher," Cora Lee piped up.

Precisely, I said.

But poor Putnam couldn't catch anything. True, he could fly, and true, he wasn't half bad at it, but he was no air witch.

"He was a *water* witch!" Cora Lee said, wiggling her feet.

And so onward he flew, following the river as it meandered northward. He flew and he flew and he flew all through the day without ever seeing any sign of another pond. He grew very hungry and tired. He had no idea where he was or where he was going. He began to second-guess this flying business.

*What am I doing?* he thought. *Why am I up here? What if I get a cramp, or my wings give out? What if I fly into a storm? Could I fly in rain? What about lightning? Or fog? Or mountains hidden inside of fog? What if I never find a new pond? Could I live in the river? Could I LAND on a river? What else lives in rivers? Do they eat grebes? Do they eat bloodworms? Do rivers have bloodworms? Do they have coots?*

And then suddenly, on the horizon, a wide field of rushes came into view. It sat a few hundred feet west of the river. The rushes swept across the area like combed tresses of golden hair. Putnam grinned. *Where there are rushes,* he thought, *there's bound to be water!*

He prepared for landing — although what that meant exactly he wasn't really sure. You see, it would be his first landing, and he was more troubled about it than he had been about his first take-off. He had no idea how to land. Should he flap his wings? Should he glide in? Should he go in feet-first? Belly-first? *Bill*-first? He leveled off and circled the area a few times, trying to make up his mind. Even if he could have decided, there was no water to land on anyway and he knew from the depth of his being that he could not land on land. (And he was right: grebes can only land on water.)

He entertained the notion of turning around and following the river back home, but he knew he'd never make it. He didn't have the strength left. He didn't have the fuel. He considered just taking his chances and landing on the river but he remembered how once he'd heard one duck saying to another how the river was very shallow in places and was also rocky and tangled with fallen branches. At the time, not really caring about the river or what it was like, he hadn't paid much attention. But now . . .

And what if he *could* land? What if the river was clear enough for him to make a safe landing? Then what? Wouldn't he still have to make his way to the rushes? The duck said the river was shallow.

Putnam needed deep water if he was going to be able to dive. So would he have to *waddle* to the rushes? He had never walked on land in his life! It seemed a bit much to have to learn both to fly and to walk in the same day! And just what exactly would he do out in the middle of a field without water to lift off from or to dive into if suddenly a predator appeared? He shuddered to think of it. *No,* he decided, *the river is out of the question.*

And then, as he was beginning his sixteenth circuit, Putnam suddenly spotted a hawk the color

of ash perched silent and still on the leafless branch of a dead cottonwood tree. Its eyes were as deep and black as an old well. They were looking in Putnam's direction.

Putnam didn't think twice. He dove for the rushes. He dove swiftly. He dove brilliantly. For diving was one thing that Putnam always put his whole self into.

*What he dove into was a cienega.*

"A what?" Cora Lee said.

It's like a marsh. Or a swamp.

"In the desert?"

Sure. They're called cienegas. The word probably came from a garbling of the Spanish expression
*cien aguas,* which means a hundred springs. Folks
are always mixing things up like that. Sometimes
they just don't pay attention.

I looked over at Cora Lee.

"I'm paying attention!" she said, scowling. "A
hundred springs! Go on!"

You see, I said, sometimes there's a layer of rock
or hard clay under the soil and so rainwater can't
seep in. It stays at the surface. In some spots,

where there are chinks in the rock or clay, water gurgles up and forms springs. There may not be a hundred of them, but there can be a lot. Grasses, like rushes and sedges, grow like crazy in a cienega. They need shallow water, and a cienega's *all* shallow water. So they cover the whole marsh.

"Are there any cienegas around here?" Cora Lee asked.

Right where we're sitting used to be part of a big one, I said. That was before the trappers came and trapped all the beavers, and the ranchers came and drained the swamps for grazing, and the river dug itself in. But parts of it have survived. I'll show you one next year when you come.

"*Bueno*," Cora Lee said, with a smile. "*Yo quiero a ver una cien aguas.*"

Translated, that meant she would like to see a hundred springs. She studies Spanish as well as penguins at school in Indiana.

Where was I? I asked.

"Putnam diving."

Right.

Maybe he just went ahead and dove because of the rushes. Or maybe he caught a glint of sunlight reflecting off the water through the tangle and, even without his being aware of it, that glint of golden light guided him in, like a lighthouse guides a ship to harbor. Whatever the reason, down he went, his wings tucked in at his sides, his feet fluttering behind him. He shut his eyes at the last second and crashed headlong into the thicket. But instead of the grasses catching him in their gentle boughs, as he'd hoped, they clawed at him with their sharp tentacles and clutched him roughly in their grip. He found himself wedged in, bill-first, like a nail in a board.

He wriggled and writhed and squirmed and beat at the rushes with his wings and his feet. He kucked and whistled and cursed. He grunted and seethed. The weeds seemed almost to tighten their grip.

*This is all the coots' fault!* Putnam told himself. *Those blasted coots! Those stupid, horrid, rotten coots! They're the reason I'm stuck here! They're the reason I'll be torn limb from limb by a hawk! It's all their fault! Stupid coots! Stupid, stupid coots! Dumb, blasted, stupid —*

"Hold on," Cora Lee said, holding up her palm. "Wait just a second."

Yes? I said, taken aback by the interruption. (I had really thrown myself into character.) What is it? I asked.

"This is starting to sound like one of those stories that's supposed to teach me something," Cora Lee said.

What do you mean? I asked innocently.

"Is this story supposed to teach me something about tolerance?"

Tolerance?

"Yeah, tolerance. My teacher talks a lot about it."

It's just a story, I said.

"I don't know," Cora Lee said. "It sounds like there's a lesson in it."

None that I'm aware of, I said.

"You sure?"

Positive.

She gave me a cool, hard look. Then she lowered her hand. "Well, all right," she said. "Go on. But just remember: I'm listening."

Fair enough, I said.

Putnam shut his eyes. *I need to calm down,* he said to himself. *I can't panic. Maybe the hawk didn't see me. I have to stop calling attention to myself. Relax.*

When he opened his eyes, he saw the rushes below him, winding and snarling and reaching downward. Through the tangle, he caught a glimpse of thick black mud. *Water!* he said to himself. He struggled and strained to reach it, but the rushes held him fast.

*If only I could reach it,* he thought, *I'd dive in as deep as I could go and stay there until the end of time, or even longer! I'd practice holding my breath until I could hold it for an hour. Then I'd only have to resurface twenty-four times a day! Maybe I could learn to hold it for TWO hours, and come up only TWELVE times a day! Or THREE hours — EIGHT times a day!*

And then suddenly, above him, the rushes

began to rustle and he heard the thrumming of wings. They beat as loudly as his heart. They drew closer. Putnam froze. He closed his eyes.

*Not again,* he said to himself.

But then, just as suddenly as it had begun, the beating stopped. A moment passed in which all Putnam heard was the wind in the weeds and the pounding of his heart. Then he opened one eye halfway and peeked back over his shoulder. Above him, perched on a reed, sat a red-winged black-bird. "Conquer-RRREEE!" it said.

"Oh!" Cora Lee sighed. "I thought for sure it was the hawk!"

Well, if it had been, I said, I guess that would've been the end of the story.

"I guess so," Cora Lee said.

But it can't be over. Pennyroyal hasn't shown up yet.

"That's right!" Cora Lee said. "When does she?"

You'll see, Cora Lee, I said.

She growled and waved me onward.

\* \* \*

Well, true to its name, the red-winged blackbird had red patches on its wings — or rather, *his* wings, for only the male of the species are black and red-winged. The females are brown. The red patches had yellow stripes at the bottom. Otherwise he looked very much like a small raven. He was smaller than Putnam. His feathers shone, black and waxy. His beak gleamed like gunmetal.

"Conquer-RRREEE!" he said again, then added, "You all right?"

Putnam breathed a sigh. "I thought you were a hawk," he said.

"CHECK!" the blackbird said. Putnam winced at the sound. "A hawk? Me? CHECK-CHECK-CHECK!" He was laughing.

Putnam had often seen — and heard — red-winged blackbirds at the pond. Their calls had always made the feathers on the back of his neck stand on end. But seeing how they were primarily shorebirds and rarely ventured out further than the rushes, and seeing how they never stole food from out of his mouth, he put up with them. Still, the nearness and sheer volume of this particular one was a little hard to bear.

"There *are* hawks around," the blackbird said, hopping down closer to Putnam's head. "Do you think nesting here is wise?"

"I'm not *nesting*," Putnam grumbled. "I'm stuck."

"Stuck? Conquer-RRREEE!"

Putnam winced.

"Here, let me help," the blackbird said, and began tugging at the rushes with his beak. He worked swiftly and deftly and in a very short time Putnam was able to move his wings. A few moments more and he was free. He scrambled to turn himself upright.

"There you go! CHECK!" the blackbird said.

Putnam clawed his way down through the grass to the mud. He dipped his bill into it and discovered it was only about two inches deep.

"Is there any *open* water around?" he asked the blackbird. "Any *deep* water?"

"Open? Deep? CHECK! Where do you think

you are? A pond? It's a cienega! CHECK! CHECK! Conquer-RRREEE!"

Putnam scowled. The water was too shallow to dive in, or even to hide in. And there was no way he could take off from it. He wasn't much better off than when he was stuck.

"There *is* some water," the blackbird said. "But I don't know how deep it is. I don't dive. I'm an icterid. Icterids don't dive."

I paused to see if I would have to explain to Cora Lee what an icterid is, but she said nothing. I went ahead and explained anyway, just in case she was afraid to ask.

The icterids, I said, are a subfamily of birds that includes —

"I know," Cora Lee said with a groan. "Blackbirds, orioles, bobolinks, and meadowlarks. They have cone-shaped beaks. You've told me a hundred times."

*American* blackbirds, I corrected.

Cora Lee shot me a glance that said, "Picky, picky, picky."

"Take me to it," Putnam said to the red-winged blackbird.

"CHECK!" the blackbird answered, and he flitted to another reed top.

Putnam scrambled after him through the rushes. He was no stranger to rushes. As far as he was concerned, rushes were the only safe place to be if you had to be above water. Safe, that is from hawks, of course, but also safe from coots. The coots rarely bothered with the rushes, preferring instead the spotlight of center pond. Putnam, on the other hand, prided himself on his knack for navigating a system of grasses, whether they be rushes, sedges, or reeds — and he knew the difference between them, believe you me. He'd spent so much time down among their roots that he'd developed a real sixth sense for the way they grew. He understood their *grain,* you might say. They seemed to almost part for him with just a nudge of his bill. Because of this, he felt a genuine fondness for them. Rushes were his friends.

But the cienega was no pond. Its grasses didn't grow modestly along the shore; they grew with abandon across the entire area, creating a massive, dense layer of matted leaves and reeds that no ordinary grebe could ever hope to penetrate. Under the water, the stalks grew so tightly together that Putnam could not make head nor tail of their origin. The water was so clogged with them that most of the time he couldn't swim, he couldn't wade — he had to walk. More than once he tripped on a strand of braided grass and fell bill-first into the muck.

Putnam decided then and there that he absolutely hated walking and swore to himself that, if he could help it, he'd never do it again, never ever, and then he cursed the coots for putting him into a situation where he had to do it in the first place.

*If there is water,* Putnam told himself, *as the blackbird says, then no matter how little there is, no matter how shallow it is, I will remain in it for the rest of my days. I shall never wander again. This I solemnly vow.*

On and on he trudged through the cienega. No matter how far he went there was always further to go, there were always more rushes to plow through, more muck to plod through, more ground to cover. And then, finally, with his feathers all ruffled and bent and broken, his legs and wings aching, his hunger burning, his will as soggy and muddied as his feet and legs, Putnam stepped into a clearing.

"This is it!" The blackbird squawked. "CHECK!"

In the clearing was a dark, murky spring about five feet across. Rushes encircled it and formed a canopy overhead. Sunlight streamed through onto the water like golden rain. Water boatmen spun on the spring's surface. A few mosquito fish nibbled them from below.

Putnam stepped cautiously into the water as if he expected some horrible cienega monster to leap out of the spring at him. But none did. He took a few more steps toward the middle. He felt his body become buoyant. He floated. What's more, the water was deep. He could feel it. It felt very deep, in fact.

"How is it?" the blackbird called out.

Putnam didn't hear him. He was too busy enjoying being on a real body of water again. It felt so soft and cool and soothing. He scooped up some water with his bill and tossed it back over his head onto his wings. He ruffled his feathers to allow it to soak in. What relief! He kicked with his feet and he turned a quick figure eight.

"CHECK!" the blackbird said. "Well, I guess I'll be off."

Again, Putnam paid him no mind. He was too intent on pressing the air and water out of his feathers in preparation to dive.

The blackbird flapped his wings and lifted off into the air. "You're welcome!" he called down as he flew away, adding, "CHECK! Conquer-RRREEE!"

Putnam didn't hear, didn't see. He had finished his preparations and was beginning to submerge, bit by bit, inch by inch, up to his neck, his chin, his bill. He lingered a second before his eyes went under, giving the cienega what he hoped would be one last look. Then he was gone.

Ohhh, it felt so good to be underwater again! He swam a brisk underwater figure eight and felt dizzy with delight. Then he dove slowly down-ward, expecting at any second to hit bottom. The water was so dark and muddy that he could barely see anything. Only golden streaks of sunlight that seemed to be following him gave him a glimpse of anything around him. They lit up a school of sil-very mosquito fish as they zigzagged by. Though Putnam was starved, he let them be. He was sure there'd be other, more savory morsels further down.

Down he dove, deeper into the blackening

spring, deeper than he'd ever been able to go in the pond, deeper than he had ever dreamed possible.

*How long have I been under?* he thought. *Has it been a minute? Two?* He wished he had counted. It had to be a record. A personal best. *I should go up for air soon,* he thought. *Just a little deeper. What could it hurt? It's so nice down here! I could stay here forever!*

And then suddenly before him, the rays of sunlight fluttered over what appeared to be a huge, black cycloptic eye. It was the blackest thing Putnam had ever seen — blacker than a diving beetle, blacker than coot feathers, blacker even than a hawk's eye. The sunrays danced in it like golden spooks. And then, as Putnam was gazing into it, hypnotized, he felt something grab him, and drag him away.

*I took out my handkerchief and wiped the lenses* of my glasses as if they had suddenly become so dirty that I couldn't see through them.

"Well?" Cora Lee asked. "What was it?"

I can't see a thing through these, I said. I don't know why I let them get so bad. Grandma is always saying, "Frank! Take out that handkerchief and wipe those filthy spectacles! What do you think it's for!"

"W-was it a cienega monster?" Cora Lee asked. She let the end of her pole dip into the water.

I put my glasses back on very slowly and then neatly folded my handkerchief and carefully tucked it back into the bib pocket of my overalls.

Then I said, as if I hadn't been listening, I'm sorry, Cora Lee, did you say something?

"Uncle Frank! *What grabbed Putnam*?!"

Suddenly, it was *Uncle* Frank.

I looked out at the water and faked a concerned expression. Cora Lee, I said, your pole's in the water. I pointed at it.

She jerked it up out of the water. The bait was gone. She gnashed her teeth. "My *name* is *Cora*!"

she snarled. "TELL ME WHAT GRABBED PUTNAM!"

Oh, *Putnam,* I said, as if I'd forgotten all about what I'd been saying. (Nieces like to think uncles forget things easily.) Putnam, Putnam, I said. Yes — the grebe story. Where was I?

"The black cycloptic eye! In the spring! In the cienega!"

Oh, of course, I said, nodding. Silly of me. I remember. Yes, the eye. It opened. Putnam was dragged away. I remember.

"Well, what was it?" Cora Lee said. She was a little annoyed with me, I think. "Was it Pennyroyal?"

Pennyroyal? I said. No, it wasn't Pennyroyal. She comes later.

"Well then, *WHAT*?" she said. She was definitely annoyed.

You'll see, Cora Lee, I said. (I never learn.)

Cora Lee's ears turned red. "Just get on with it!" she snarled. She jerked in her pole and plucked a worm from out of the worm can.

You really shouldn't worm when you're upset, I

said. At least that's what Grandpa always says. "Never worm when you're upset," he always told me.

Cora Lee glared at me. I could have sworn I saw steam coming out of her ears.

I'll get on with it, I said.

The next thing Putnam knew he was rising up out of the black water, bit by bit. First came his crown, dark and shimmery like the back of a baby box turtle, then his pied bill, short and gray and chick-enlike (it looked like it had been tied shut), then his zebra-striped head, his black throat, his brown breast, the white puff where his tail ought to have been. The whole grebe. His dark eyes squinted in the gloom.

He was no longer in the cienega. He was not under the canopy of rushes. He was at the water's surface, but he knew somehow that he was not aboveground. He was underground. Putnam always knew which way was up.

He surveyed his new surroundings, paddling lightly, turning his head constantly from side to side as grebes are wont to do. It was very dark, the only light being the faint golden glow of sunshine that had followed him from the spring. It flickered dimly in the water, trapped like a firefly between two cupped hands. His eyes adjusted quickly to the darkness. Diving birds are used to dark places. Soon he could see as well as if it were midday on the pond. He found that he was in a pool of water inside a stone chamber of some sort. An underground cave is what it was. The ceiling was low, just a few feet above his head. The walls of the cave were gray and bare. There were nooks and crannies and cubbies cut into them along the water's surface, like little coves. As Putnam paddled around, he peered into one. He thought he saw the shape of a bird slowly sinking into the water, grebe-style, then he heard a *blump*!

Putnam tried to piece together what had happened — how he had arrived at the cave — but his memory was a little patchy. He remembered crashing into the cienega. He remembered being stuck, bill-first. He remembered following the red-winged blackbird through the rushes. He remembered diving down into the spring and the shafts of golden sunlight. He remembered the school of mosquito fish swimming by. He remembered feeling as if he should turn back, that he'd been down too long, but that he had been unwilling to, almost determined not to. After that his memory got hazy.

He vaguely remembered a circle, a black circle, like an eye — a grebe eye, that is — opening up. Then something grabbed him — he didn't know what. It pulled him. He didn't remember fighting it. Maybe he just had no fight left after the day he'd had. Maybe he just didn't care anymore. He remembered wondering if maybe he was drowning and if the pull he felt was his life being taken away. Then he blacked out.

When he came to, he was still underwater. He assumed he was in the spring and quickly darted upward. As disoriented as he was, he knew the way up. He always did. When he reached the surface, he looked around to find himself in the underground pool. In the cave.

\*　　\*　　\*

Putnam heard a plash behind him. It echoed around the cave. He sunk into the water up to his chin and turned slowly around to find mosquito fish scouring the surface for food. Now, as I've mentioned, mosquito fish were not anywhere near the top of Putnam's favorite snack list. They weren't even near the bottom. But Putnam had had a very trying, tiring day, and the truth was, he was famished. He wasn't about to be finicky. He'd eat what was in front of him. He sank slowly below the surface and struck at one of the mosquito fish, catching it in his bill. Then he brought it back up to the surface and gulped it down. His face soured.

*Ew!* he thought. *Bitter!*

Then, having had his appetizer — unappetizing as it was — he dove for the bottom in hopes of finding a main course: some snails maybe, or larvae, or perhaps even some juicy, red bloodworms. But he couldn't find it. The bottom, I mean. He dove as deep as he could, deeper than he'd ever gone, but he never reached it. *Maybe there is no bottom,* he thought.

He also found no food: no snails, no larvae, no bloodworms, no nothing. The pool was lifeless, aside, of course, from himself and the mosquito fish. Just his dumb luck.

He swam back up to the surface and he sat upon the water in the center of the pool — there being no rushes for him to hide in. His stomach grumbled out loud, echoing its discontent around the cave. Putnam considered catching another mosquito fish. His stomach voted yes. His tongue voted no. In the end, his stomach won out. Taste is no match for a growling belly. He snatched up another of the minnows. This time, before swallowing, he carried it beneath the surface in his bill, thinking, even if it meant gulping some water, it would still be better to eat it while holding his breath. You don't taste as much that way, you know.

"That's how I eat brussels sprouts," Cora Lee said with a nod.

Me, too, I said.

Putnam then resurfaced and snatched another minnow. He carried it underwater and ate it, too.

Then he caught another. He ate five in all. When finally his belly was full, he sat on the surface of the pool, preening himself. He plucked out bent and broken feathers. He rolled the top of his head against his back, then shook like a dog after a bath. His feathers fluffed up. He combed them back down with his bill and gave them one final going over. Then at last, feeling much more himself again, and feeling safe and alone in the cave, he tucked his bill into his wing and slept.

When he awoke, he discovered that he was not alone at all — not in the slightest. He looked around to see that in nearly every nook and cranny and cubby of the cave sat a water bird. He sank down into the water up to his neck, and, periscopelike, scanned the scene. The birds in the nook, crannies, and cubbies did the same.

"They're pied-billeds," Cora Lee said.

They were indeed, I said. Except that their bills weren't pied. You see, in the winter, the band on the pied-billed grebe's bill fades. Its throat also changes — from black to white. This happens when the days grow shorter, when there's less light.

Down in the cave, where there was hardly *any* light, the grebes' bodies were tricked into thinking winter had come and changed accordingly. They became *un*pied-billed pied-billed grebes.

"So did Putnam lose his band, too?" Cora Lee asked.

In time, I said. His throat turned white, too. He assumed, as the others had, that it meant autumn had ended. He couldn't know that he'd entered a kind of perpetual winter, or how long the other grebes had been down there.

He didn't attempt to speak to any of them. He wouldn't have liked it if they had rushed up to him asking a bunch of silly questions — which they didn't; they stayed in their places, like good grebes, and left Putnam alone to sort things out on his own.

The way Putnam had it figured, they must have all arrived in the cave the same way he had: they must have all left home and crashed into the cienega; they must have all tromped through the rushes to the spring; they must have all dived in and been dragged down by the pull into the cavern. Supposing the grebes had arrived in some other way — what possible difference could it make? They were all there. They weren't going anywhere. And none of them seemed to be all that worked up about it.

And so Putnam gave up thinking about the hows and whys of it all, figuring that wherever he was and however he got there and whatever the Sam Hill was going on, this was his new home, whether he liked it or not. He paddled over to the cave wall. The grebes all sank in their coves. He found himself a nice, unoccupied cubby, and settled in.

The grebes never once spoke, to him or to one another. They all just kept their distance. Mostly, they stayed in their places. They must have crept out and dove sometimes, but Putnam never saw them do it. One minute there would be a grebe tucked into a cranny, the next, there was not. Occasionally, one of them would surface with a mosquito fish in its bill and swallow it. Their faces would always sour.

*They should do it underwater,* Putnam thought.

Putnam sometimes partook of mosquito fish as well, but only when he had to, only when his hunger got the best of him. They were the bitterest fish he'd ever had to swallow. Still, at least there was always plenty of them.

Putnam couldn't say for sure where they had all come from. He never saw them spawn. There were never baby mosquito fish. But he had formed a theory.

Putnam wasn't the last grebe to appear in the cave. New grebes were showing up all the time. Each time one arrived the same thing happened: First there was a dim flash of golden light in the water, and then a poor, confused grebe rose up out of it, bit by bit, looking around nervously. Then he or she (and there's no real effective way — for us anyhow — to tell he-grebes from she-grebes, though *they* seem to manage well enough) would dive below the surface and return with a mosquito fish in his or her beak. He or she would gulp it down, make a sour face, pick out a nice nook or cranny to call his or her own, and settle in. Then things would quiet back down — at least until the next one arrived.

What Putnam found curious about all of this was that each time a new grebe arrived, suddenly — Poof! — there were more mosquito fish in the pool. It was his belief that the grebes and the minnows all got pulled in together.

"Sounds reasonable," Cora Lee said.

Time went on, although down there you'd never know it. Putnam passed through another molt and lost his zebra stripes altogether. He was now brown and drab, save his white throat and the white puff where his tail ought to have been.

He often sat on the water in his cubby, closing his eyes and imagining his pond, far away and above. He imagined the sun. He imagined the rushes. He imagined the water bugs, the froglets, the larvae, and the bloodworms. He missed having a choice. But he also imagined, with a shudder, the vultures and the ravens and the hawks — and the coots! *At least I've escaped them,* he told himself. *I've escaped them all.*

When Putnam tired of brooding, he'd sink slowly under the surface — provided no one was watching, of course — and dive. He let go of his memories, good and bad and in between, and delighted in the extraordinary depth of the pool. The water was as deep as any grebe could ever hope for. Putnam had plumbed the pool's depths many times but had never reached anything of substance, had never been able to say to himself, *There! That's the bottom!* and push off it. In one sense, this was deeply troubling to him. *Things should have a bottom,* he often thought to himself. *They just should.* But in another, more mysterious and somewhat exciting way, it thrilled him. Alone, down in the vast blue-black swirl, he felt as if he were no longer a part of this world, that he had somehow escaped all earthly things forever.

Until his breath ran out.

In time, Putnam thought less and less of the pond and came to regard the underground cave as, if not exactly home, then, at the very least, a safe, peaceful, predictable place to live.

And then came Pennyroyal.

"*Fi*-nally!" Cora Lee said.

*Are you hungry? I asked Cora Lee.*

I reached for my lunch pail. Want some lunch?

"Lunch?" she said. "No! I want to hear about Pennyroyal!"

I brought your favorite: liverwurst on rye.

"*My* favorite! That's *your* favorite!"

Really? I said, popping open the lunch pail. What do you like?

"Frank!" Cora Lee barked. She snatched the lunch pail from me and snapped it shut. "You can eat later! Get back to the story!"

No lunch? I said as pathetically as I could.

"Later!" she said. "After the story! Tell me about Pennyroyal!"

How about a corner? I said. Couldn't you just tear me off a little corner?

Cora Lee set the lunch pail on the other side of her — far away from me.

"Pennyroyal," she said tersely, pointing her finger at me, "then liverwurst." She tapped the lunch pail with her finger.

She got that from her grandma. My mother always used liverwurst as bait, too.


Pennyroyal rose up out of the water as all the other grebes before her had done — bit by bit. First came her crown, dark and shimmery like a baby box turtle's back. Then the bill. Her bill was the first thing about Pennyroyal that Putnam found odd. It was not chickenlike. It was black and long and pointed, like a loon's, like a dagger. And it was not pied. Next came her black throat, her brown breast, the white puff where her tail ought to have been. The whole grebe. Her golden eyes opened wide, blazing in the gloom.

"*Golden* eyes?" Cora Lee said, looking up at me.

That was the second odd thing, I said.

Pennyroyal dove and quickly resurfaced with a mosquito fish in her beak. She gulped it down. Her face soured.

"Ew!" she groaned. "Bitter!"

Putnam nodded in his cubby.

Pennyroyal paddled around the pool, turning her head from side to side and peering into the nooks and crannies and cubbies. When she neared Putnam's, he shrank back and sank down up to his bill.

"I just don't understand this," Pennyroyal said to herself. "What kind of pond *is* this?"

*Pond?* Putnam thought. Why, even he had never considered the place — whatever it was — to be a *pond.*

*After all,* he thought, *there are no cattails, no water lilies. There's not even any duckweed. There's only the cold stone and the empty water — empty except for us, and the mosquito fish.*

*What do THEY eat?* Putnam suddenly wondered. *There aren't any mosquitoes. There's no algae or water bugs. But I do see them feeding on the surface.*

"There must be food too small for him to see," Cora Lee said. "Microscopic food. Like protozoa."

I nodded. Such a clever girl.

"You!" Pennyroyal suddenly shouted.

"You! You!" her echo repeated.

Putnam snapped out of his thoughts to find Pennyroyal staring directly at him, her eyes shining like twin suns. He dove. Bill-first.

As he made his way down through the dark, cool water, he thought of the steady stream of grebes that he had watched rise up out the pool since he himself had come up out of it, heaven knows how long ago. He couldn't really even guess how many of them there had been, but he would not have been surprised to learn there were fifty, or a hundred — maybe two hundred. There was just no way of knowing. One thing he did know, however, was that, be there ten or ten thousand, up to then exactly *none* of them had ever spoken to him before. Certainly, none had ever rushed up shouting "You!"

Not until Pennyroyal, that is. She and her pointy bill and her golden eyes — she was changing everything.

She certainly was persistent. She approached every grebe she saw. "You!" was all she usually got out before the grebe ducked out of sight.

"Well, I never!" she always said. "Queek, queek, queek!"

Nevertheless, on she chased and chased and chased, and on they ducked and ducked and dove. None of the grebes ever answered her. None of them ever listened. But Pennyroyal never gave up. She never gave them a moment's peace. She knew they had to come up sometime, so she sat on the surface and waited.

Once, as Putnam was resurfacing from a long dive, he heard a voice from behind him.

"Excuse me," it said. "Can you tell me how to get out of here?"

Putnam spun around to find Pennyroyal sitting

on the water less than a foot away, her golden eyes
half open. They looked blurry, unfocused. Putnam
had been under far too long to dive again so soon.
He had no breath left. So he just sank down into
the water as far as he could.

"Please," she said, paddling closer. "I don't
know where I am and I can't find my way out." A
golden tear sprouted in her eye and ran down her
cheek to her neck, then down over her breast and
into the black water.

Putnam back-paddled.

"My name is Pennyroyal Grebe," Pennyroyal
said. "What's yours?"

Finally, Putnam managed to catch his breath.
He held it and sank from sight. He heard sad,
muffled queeking above.

*This has to stop,* Putnam told himself as he dove. *It's gotten so a grebe can't even go up for air without being pounced upon. She's upsetting the balance is what she's doing. Upsetting the balance. She has to be stopped. She's ruining everything.*

He passed through a school of mosquito fish, which quickly broke ranks and shot off in every direction. Then, without intending to, without really thinking about it, he lunged at one and caught it. He didn't know why. He wasn't hungry at all. He'd eaten only the day before. But there he was, with a minnow in his mouth. Then, as if that weren't odd enough, instead of gobbling it down underwater as he always did, he carried it to the surface. Again, he wasn't sure why. He swallowed the fish, and grimaced.

"They're bitter," a voice from the dark said.

Putnam turned to see Pennyroyal emerging from a dark cubby. It was *his* cubby. He began to submerge. When he was up to his chin in the water, however, he stopped. He wasn't sure why.

He was doing a lot of things he didn't understand.

"It's me again," Pennyroyal said.

*Pennyroyal Grebe,* Putnam thought. *But what sort of grebe? A golden-eyed, pointy-billed, PUSHY grebe?* He sank lower. Only his eyes and crown showed.

"Don't go!" Pennyroyal pleaded. "Please! Won't you help me?"

*Help you?* Putnam thought. *Help? Help how? What can I do? What do I know? Why can't you just be like the others? Why are you fighting? Why are you the way you are instead of the way WE are?*

*And why won't you just leave me alone?*

"There's a way in," Pennyroyal said. "So there has to be a way out. How do I get out of here?"

*There's no way out of here,* Putnam thought.

"I think I understand," she said, squinting slightly and leaning in closer. Putnam backed away. "You don't know, do you?"

Putnam felt his bill moving ever so slightly from side to side, although he hadn't willed it to do so.

"None of you know," Pennyroyal went on, moving closer still. Putnam could see his reflection in her eyes, one in each golden circle. "If you knew, you'd go yourselves." She stopped. "Wouldn't you?" She seemed to be posing this question to herself.

Suddenly, Putnam wondered why he was still there. A flee mechanism pounded in his temples as if a hawk were dropping from the sky on him.

But still he stayed.

Pennyroyal edged in farther. She leaned over so that their bills were only an inch apart.

*She is a very small grebe,* Putnam thought. He hadn't noticed before.

"You don't want to go," she said with a queer smile.

Putnam vanished beneath the surface.

*It was clear now to Putnam that Pennyroyal* was his mortal enemy, just as a hawk or any other bird of prey was — maybe more so. He decided that whatever sort of grebe she was she wasn't the sort of grebe he was, and she was probably the sort of grebe that should be avoided by the sort of grebe he was. He even began to doubt that she was a grebe at all. What had made him jump to that conclusion anyway? Because she rose from the water bit by bit? Because she was brown? Because she was a bird and was *there?* After all, until she came, there were only grebes and mosquito fish. It made sense that Putnam would just assume that she was the former. She was clearly not the latter. His reasoning had been sound. Everything seemed to point to Pennyroyal being a grebe. He couldn't be blamed for judging rashly. He couldn't be blamed for jumping to conclusions. *Anyone else,* he told himself, *would have done the same.*

And, besides, she did give her name as Pennyroyal Grebe. What of that? Putnam had heard tell of birds that sometimes ape the calls of other birds.

"Chats," Cora Lee said with a nod. "And mockingbirds."

Exactly, I said.

*And why,* Putnam thought, *would a bird pretend to be another bird? Why would a bird that is not a grebe say that she is? The answer,* he thought, *is obvious. She's up to something.*

He decided that he had better keep an eye on her. *Know your enemies,* he told himself. *Know them well.* He would note how she behaved, check her for signs of grebeness, look for lapses in her little act. For example, does she swim underwater in figure eights? Are her toes lobed? Does she eat her own feathers? He would watch her day and night (although down there he had no way of knowing which was which). *You can't be too careful,* he thought.

He rose slowly to the surface. He stopped when his black eyes appeared above the water. He rolled them left. He rolled them right. He turned his head slowly around and scanned the scene behind him. No Pennyroyal.

*I was so clever not to tell her my name!* he thought. He had been tempted. If he had told her, he felt sure that she would have hatched some devilish scheme. He had been wise to keep his bill shut. He made a solemn vow to keep it shut from then on.

Then, moving so slowly that he barely stirred the surface of the pool, he paddled softly forward, peering into nooks and crannies and cubbies. He found no one.

"Grebe!" a voice kucked from behind him. It was Pennyroyal's voice.

"Cow!" Putnam croaked and dove, bill-first, into the water.

His heart pounded as he plunged. Had she read his thoughts? Had she been reading them all along? A shiver ran down his spine.

*It's the eyes!* he thought. *Those golden eyes! What sort of grebe has golden eyes?!*

*Oh, why did she come!* he lamented. *Why won't she leave! She is noisome and bothersome and meddlesome — more like a COOT than a grebe!*

*A COOT! Of course! That would explain everything!* Putnam told himself. *She must be a COOT! It adds up! Coots have sharp bills! Coots even have lobed feet! You'd never catch a grebe kicking up a fuss the way she's always doing! You'd never catch a grebe barking and honking from the center of a pool! A grebe knows its place. A grebe is content to remain modestly off in the rushes, diving for food and minding its own business. But a coot thinks the pond owes him a living. A coot coasts along the surface, dabbling idly in the water, waiting for its food to come to him. And of course it does, just as soon as a hardworking grebe brings up a caddis nymph or a froglet it has hunted for and labored after and, finally, triumphed over. Then the coot just swipes it away and swallows it and sets into cackling — 'BWAAK, BWAAK, BWAAK!' — leaving the humble grebe to*

*dive back down to the bottom, and settle for snails.*
*There are, of course, no more bloodworms.*

*Pennyroyal GREBE,* he thought. *She is nothing*
*of the kind! Pennyroyal COOT, more like!*

"Is Pennyroyal a *coot*?" Cora Lee asked, sounding a
little disappointed.

Would it matter?

"But I feel sorry for her."

Couldn't you feel sorry for her if she were a
coot?

Cora Lee thought about this a minute, then she
looked out at the coots on the pond. They were
dabbling. "I don't know," she said. "At least she
isn't like Putnam, I guess."

You don't like Putnam? I said a bit defensively.

"He's a chicken," Cora Lee said.

A grebe, I said.

"You know what I mean. He should speak up
sometimes." She got quiet again, looked out at the
coots. "I don't think she's a coot," she said softly.
"Maybe she's a loon." She sighed.

A few quiet moments passed. The story disposition returned. So I went on:

Time went by as it always did underground — unmarked. Pennyroyal became pushier and pushier, and peevisher and peevisher. It got to the point that no grebe could sit idly upon the water in his or her own little nook or cranny or cubby and just mind his or her business without being attacked by a mad coot. The situation was, to

Putnam's mind, absolutely untenable. *Something,* he said to himself, *must be done.*

He thought and he thought and he thought but could come up with only one solution: he was going to have to reach the bottom of the pool. Somehow he knew that the bottom held the key. He couldn't say what the key was — maybe it was a way out, maybe it was just bloodworm — but the bottom beckoned and he was determined to find it.

He began training. In no time he was staying under for over two minutes. But that wasn't long enough. The bottom was more than two minutes deep. He dove again and again and again, each dive adding seconds to his time — one hundred and thirty seconds, one hundred thirty-five, one forty. Still no bottom. He kept on. One forty-five, one fifty, one fifty-five. And on.

As he trained, he made sure to check on Pennyroyal periodically, to see what she was up to. More and more all she was up to was floating sullenly on the surface. The grebes had gotten so good at avoiding her that she was finding herself with fewer and fewer opportunities to attack. She was becoming despondent. She looked thin and sickly.

Putnam found all this gratifying. He ate more mosquito fish than ever. He had to keep up his strength. The mosquito fish, by the way, didn't seem to taste as bitter as before.

A month later, in the dead of winter, Putnam came splashing up out of the pool, gasping for breath and panting, "Three minutes! Three minutes!" He swam a few quick laps in search of a witness but found no one.

Where was Pennyroyal? Lately he could always find her floating still in a certain little dark cubby that used to be his but that she had claimed for herself. But she wasn't there. Maybe she was diving. Maybe she had been following him!

But then he noticed a bird lying on its side up on a stone ledge that overlooked the pool. The bird's lobed feet dangled over the edge, the tips of its toes touching the water. Putnam had never seen one of the cave grebes climb up out of the pool before. It wasn't like a grebe to voluntarily leave the water. *Maybe it's not a grebe,* he thought.

The bird didn't move as Putnam paddled in closer. Its head was tucked under its wing on the far side of its body. Putnam examined its feet. They were lobed, and a bit smaller than his. They lacked the hooked claws of a coot — the scallops. They were grebe feet: lobed and unscalloped.

Putnam clambered up onto the ledge. The bird still hadn't moved. Putnam was fairly sure that it was dying, or had died. He waddled around to the other side of it and nosed in close. The bird's breast was ever so lightly rising and falling. It was alive.

He nudged the bird with his bill. The bird gave a shudder and slowly withdrew its head from under its wing. Its bill wasn't pied. It wasn't short. It wasn't chickenlike. It was thin and pointy.

And then the bird opened its eyes. Its golden eyes.

*"It was Pennyroyal?" Cora Lee asked, sounding* worried. "Was she all right?"

Well, she'd seen better days. Her feathers were a mess — splintered and unpreened. Her eyes were not so much like the sun anymore. They were more like rushes in autumn — golden, but faded.

Putnam looked deep into them. They did not seem to be looking back. A chill ran down his spine. Had she just this second gone?

"Pennyroyal," he whispered. It was the first word he'd ever spoken to her. He nudged her again. She didn't move. His heart was pounding in his ears. "Pennyroyal," he repeated a little louder.

"Pennyroyal, royal," his echo answered.

He detected movement out of the corners of his

eye and heard the faint lapping of water. When he turned he saw for a moment the shadowy outlines of a multitude of birds before they shrank back into the darkness. When he turned back to Pennyroyal, her eyes were gazing up at him.

"You," she said weakly.

Putnam was so startled he staggered back a few steps and slipped off the ledge into the pool. He poked his head back up out of the water, periscopelike, and looked up at her.

"How can you live like this?" she asked him. She paused between her words as if it took great strength to get them out, as if each one weighed a ton.

Putnam felt a pang of guilt in his belly. He regretted feeling glad that she had become sickly and thin. He regretted feeling gratified by her unhappiness. He never wanted her to die. He just wanted her to go.

"Y-you should eat," he said, his words surprising even himself.

He dove, caught a mosquito fish, and brought it back to the surface. He laid it carefully on the ledge beside her, then slipped back down into the water.

The minnow didn't flop about. It sat very still, gazing up at Pennyroyal, as if resigned to its fate.

"Go on," Putnam said to her. "They're not as bitter as they used to be."

The fish looked over at Putnam, then up at Pennyroyal. Then, it slowly began to inch away toward the ledge. Putnam rose up and nudged it back with his bill. The minnow sighed.

Pennyroyal closed her eyes. She opened her bill to talk but "Why?" was all that came out.

"Why?" Putnam replied. "Why, to *live*," he said.

"Why live?" Pennyroyal said, her eyes still closed.

"To leave," Putnam said. "So you can leave."

Pennyroyal laughed without opening her bill. The sound came out through her nostrils. Her eyes opened and she glared at Putnam. "Leave?" she said. "Leave how?"

Putnam wished he knew. Her leaving was his only hope of life regaining any sort of normalcy. It was her only hope, perhaps, of surviving. The cave was killing her. But Putnam didn't know the way out. Pennyroyal had once said there had to be a way: where there's a way in, there's a way out.

Putnam thought of the day he had sunk to the bottom of the pond — the first day out of his shell. It had seemed to him then, as he lay there in the mud, that there was no way out and that his life was doomed to brevity. He knew then how he had gotten into that mess. He knew the "way in." But it didn't do him much good. It sure didn't help him get out.

And then there was the time he got stuck bill-first in the cienega. He certainly knew the way in then, too, but it didn't do him any good either. He began to wonder about Pennyroyal's theory about ways in and out. *Maybe,* he thought, *you could get into something and never get out of it, no matter how you got there.*

But then it dawned on him that he *did* get out of those scrapes. He *didn't* drown on the pond floor. He *didn't* get eaten by a hawk in the rushes. All those times he had found a way out! *How?* he thought. *How did I get out?*

"With help," he said to Pennyroyal, smiling. "I'll help you."

Pennyroyal would eat nothing except her feathers.

"You have to eat," Putnam told her, nudging the fish closer to her.

"No!" Pennyroyal groaned, rolling away. "They're disgusting!"

The minnow smiled. It started edging itself toward the ledge.

Putnam waddled around Pennyroyal and looked in her eyes. "You have to eat," he said. "It's a little one." It was about seven-eighths of an inch long. "Eat it quickly," Putnam said. "One gulp. Don't even think about it. Hold your breath. Think about something else. Think about, um . . . I know! Think about bloodworms!" He smiled.

"Yuck!" Pennyroyal groaned. "I hate bloodworms!"

*She just can't be a grebe,* Putnam thought.

"Then think of larvae," he suggested.

"What kind?" Pennyroyal said with a squint.

"Any kind! What's your favorite?"

"Caddis," she answered, brightening a little.

"Then think of caddis nymphs," Putnam said. "Crunchy and delicious."

Pennyroyal looked down at the fish. It had almost reached the ledge. "Oh, okay," she whined. She closed her eyes.

Putnam scooped up the fish and spooned it into her mouth.

"Crunchy and delicious," Putnam said as the fish slid down her throat.

Pennyroyal's face soured. "Blecch!" she said.

"You just need to concentrate harder," Putnam said. He fetched another fish, this one an inch and a quarter.

"No!" Pennyroyal said, waving a wing. "No more fish!"

"This isn't a fish," Putnam said, lying the mosquito fish beside her. "It's a caddis nymph."

The mosquito fish shot Putnam a puzzled look.

Pennyroyal groaned but picked up the fish anyway. She closed her golden eyes. The fish closed its eyes, too. Pennyroyal gulped it down.

"Well?" Putnam said.

"Crunchy," she lied.

"And?"

She scowled at him. "Delicious."

"Good," he said. "One more." He dove before she could object.

After Pennyroyal had downed her fourth mosquito fish — a two-and-a-half incher — she said to Putnam, "How do you do it?"

"I eat them underwater," Putnam said.

"No, I mean, how do you live down here?" Pennyroyal said. "How do you keep your spirits up?"

Putnam looked away. He saw several silhouetted grebe heads poking up out of the water. They disappeared with a *blump!*

"Don't you want to leave?" she asked.

Putnam climbed down into the water and sank down to his chin.

"Wouldn't you like to go home?" she asked.

Putnam sank lower. Only his eyes and crown showed.

"Someplace new then!" Pennyroyal said, her

eyes gleaming. They seemed to brighten the cave. "Wouldn't you like to go on an *adventure!*"

*I've had my share of adventure,* Putnam thought to himself.

"That's how I got here," Pennyroyal said, a little glumly.

Putnam rose up an inch. He felt a tug in his belly. A tug of excitement. *We were both on adventures!* he thought. *We're ADVENTURERS!*

"W-would you t-tell me about it?" he said excitedly. "P-please?"

The other grebes leaned forward in their places.

Pennyroyal shut her eyes. "Another time," she murmured. "I'm bushed." She climbed down from the ledge and sat on the water. She opened a wing and tucked her head inside.

Putnam and the other grebes gathered silently around her as she slept. They sat on the surface together for the first time, none of them diving, none of them sinking, none retreating to their nooks and crannies and cubbies. Putnam was surprised at how many of them there were — they nearly covered the pool. They must have been surprised as well, judging from the way they all kept looking shyly from one to another. Putnam saw that none of them, not even the new arrivals, had bands on their bills. *But,* he thought, *they're all pied-billeds just the same.*

*Cora Lee reached beside her and lifted my* lunch pail up onto her lap. She opened it, removed two sandwiches wrapped in aluminum foil, and handed one to me.

"Now you can eat," she said.

I took the sandwich and began unwrapping it.

"No sandwich bags again?" Cora Lee asked as she opened hers. She lifted the top slice of bread and peeked under it. Her nose wrinkled. She put the bread back down and looked up at me. "What is liverwurst anyway?" she asked.

It's a sausage, I told her. A liver sausage. But this is liverwurst spread.

"So it's *mashed* liver sausage?" Cora Lee said with a shiver.

It's best not to think too much about it, I said. But it's good for you. It's loaded with iron.

"I'm sure," Cora Lee said.

She rewrapped the sandwich and put it back in the lunch pail, then took out the thermos and an apple. The thermos was filled with chocolate milk — her favorite. She unscrewed the cup from the top and set it on the ground between us. Then she poured some of the creamy brown liquid into it.

It's chocolate milk, I said smiling. Your favorite.

"My favorite is peppermint tea," she said. "I grew out of chocolate milk years ago."

I didn't realize, I said.

She took a sip from her cup and frowned slightly.

"That was about the same time that I grew out of apples," she said.

Grew out of apples? I said. I didn't know people grew out of apples.

"Well, I did," Cora Lee said. She took a bite of the apple anyway — so I wouldn't feel bad, I suppose.

I'll drink it, I said, reaching out my hand. I still like chocolate milk.

"Oh, I'll drink it," she said, guarding her cup with her free arm. "It's just not my favorite, that's all."

She poured chocolate milk into the extra cup and handed it to me, then we sat silently awhile, enjoying our picnic. I have always been partial to

eating in silence. That way I focus better on what I'm eating, how it tastes. I've never been one to eat while reading, or watching television, or driving. That doesn't make sense to me. You'd never see any other animal doing that. I have also always been partial to eating outdoors. To me, the best moment of any fishing trip or campout or hike is the breaking out of the grub. There is something about fresh air and wilderness that makes any food taste better. Even mashed liver sausage spread sandwiches.

Cora Lee finished her apple and the store-bought oatmeal-raisin cookies I'd packed and then, while I was thinking about how and where I prefer eating, she snuck into the lunch pail again and took the sandwich back out. She set it beside her on the ground and quietly unwrapped the foil. I pretended not to notice. With her head turned away, she tore off bits of the sandwich and discreetly popped them into her mouth. I waited until her mouth was full, then asked, "Can I have an apple?" She covered her mouth with her hand

and with the other took out the second apple from the pail and passed it to me.

What do you eat now that you've outgrown them? I asked.

She chewed as quickly as she could, gulped audibly, then sputtered, "Persimmons."

Persimmons?

"Mm-hm," she said, taking a sip of what used to be her favorite beverage. "Mama gets them for me at this fancy produce stand in Michigan City. They're Japanese, you know."

Oh, I know, I said. I took a bite from my apple and wondered what a persimmon even looked like.

When lunch was over and our trash tucked away in the lunch pail, Cora Lee wormed her hook, cast her line, and told me to continue the story.

Do you remember where we were? I asked.

"Pennyroyal's resting on the water with all the pied-billeds around her, waiting for her to wake up and tell them all about her adventure."

I was glad one of us remembered.

*   *   *

Well, I said, when Pennyroyal awoke, she turned to Putnam and said, "I'm a least grebe. We don't usually come this far north."

*"Least"?* Putnam thought. *What could that mean? Why "least"? Were they rare? Were they weak? Could they dive deep? Could they dive? What was wrong with them that they should be called "least"?*

But then he looked at her with all the other grebes sitting around her, and saw how small she was — she really was small; she sure didn't act small — and he knew why.

"I don't really like the 'least' part," Pennyroyal went on. "I'm not even so crazy about the 'grebe' part. I prefer water witch."

"Wait a minute," Cora Lee interrupted. "I thought you said *pied-billed* grebes were called water witches. Are least grebes water witches, too?"

Not really, I said. But Pennyroyal always liked having the last word over what folks called her.

Cora Lee gave me a look that meant she knew what I was getting at, then said, "Okay, *Francis.*"

"I thought you were a coot," Putnam said.

Pennyroyal gave a little laugh. "Would that have been so bad?"

Putnam shrugged. He didn't like to speak badly of others. He wouldn't like it done of him. But surely if she had ever met a coot, she would never have asked that question.

"I met up with some coots just before I came here," she told him. "On a pond near a little river. They were very friendly."

*A pond near a river?* Putnam thought.

"It was a very nice little pond, surrounded by cottonwoods and willows. I spent a few days there just sitting with them out on the middle," she said. "It was very beautiful from there."

*I wouldn't know,* Putnam thought.

"They had me in stitches most of the time! Once —" She had to stop due to a mild fit of laughter. "Once," she went on when it had passed, "they told me this very funny story about a loon —" She laughed again, harder, forcing a large percentage of the grebes underwater. "This loon," she went on, "flew straight into —" (laughter) "into a fog —" (more laughter) "and ran straight into a —" (big laugh) "a mountain!" At this she rocked so hard she tipped over backward.

*Sounds painful,* Putnam said to himself. He glanced around at the remaining grebes. A few of them were suppressing snickers.

"Oh!" Pennyroyal squeaked as she pulled herself upright. "And they told me about this *grebe,* this poor, meek little grebe, that was so anxious to be-friend them that he would often catch food and offer it to them! Then he would just slip back under the water without a word!" Again her glee overtook her and she rolled over backward. "The coots laughed and laughed," she said. "He wanted their friendship enough to fish for them, but was too shy to even manage a hello! Then, one day, he just up and flew away. As he flew over, he called down to them, 'Catch your own food from now on!'" She tried to laugh but by then she was so tired that just a few wheezy queeks came out. She took a deep breath and let it out. "Funny birds," she sighed, shaking her head. "Funny, funny birds."

*They lie!* Putnam said to himself. *I never caught food for them! They STOLE it, brazenly, and with malice in their hearts. True, I often heard them laughing above afterward, but it was not at my meekness that they laughed; it was at their own wickedness.*

It didn't surprise him that they had twisted the story to make him out to look ridiculous. But it did make him angry that Pennyroyal was out spreading their lies far and wide. Still, he didn't protest. *Protesting,* he thought, *would only make me seem petty. Let her believe what she wants. It's enough that I know the truth.*

"If you were having such fun, why did you leave?" Putnam asked a bit sarcastically.

"Oh, I don't know," Pennyroyal said. "I like leaving. Going on adventures. Besides, some turkey vultures said I might enjoy the cienega just up the river. I had never seen one before. A cienega, I mean."

*Turkey vultures?* Putnam thought. *She asked advice of turkey vultures? And they spoke to her? Turkey vultures don't speak. At best they grunt!*

"I chatted awhile with them and asked if they knew where I might find water for diving. They were really very helpful, though I have to admit I had to just about pull the words out of their mouths. They're not really big talkers, are they?"

Putnam just shrugged. He honestly couldn't say.

"Now, ravens — they're another matter completely!" Pennyroyal said. "They'll cluck their tongues all day if you let them. I caught up with a few of them flying north over the river. They seemed to know the area like the backs of their claws. Very clever. A little intimidating, though, don't you think?"

Again Putnam shrugged.

"They said I should follow them out over the desert to a quaint little mountain spring they knew. That was how they described it: 'a quaint little mountain spring.' But I knew better. Ravens are clever. Maybe a little too clever. You know what I mean?"

"I guess so," Putnam said.

"I get the feeling they're not so sincere. Like they don't say what's on their minds. Sometimes I think too much cleverness isn't such a good thing."

Putnam said nothing. He reached back and bit off a billful of down and chewed it.

"Anyway, we parted ways and later I met up with a flycatcher. Beautiful bird. As red as blood. And an amazing hunter. While I flew with him he caught dozens of flying insects. Not just flies, either. That's a bit of a misnomer, flycatcher is. He caught bees and damselflies, even a grasshopper. It was as big as he was!"

Putnam remembered the red flycatcher he'd seen. The bird hadn't seemed very interested in giving him the time of day, and so Putnam hadn't given it either.

"And then I arrived at the cienega," Pennyroyal said a bit pensively. "There was a hawk in a tree."

*"A hawk?" Putnam asked.*

"Yes," Pennyroyal said. "A hawk."

"A gray hawk?"

"I think so. Yes."

"In a dead tree? A dead *cottonwood* tree?"

"That's right."

"Did it see you?"

"I flew over to it."

"*You flew over to it!*" Putnam gasped.

"Of course."

"Why?"

"To ask a question."

"Of a hawk?"

"Yes!" Pennyroyal said, laughing. "What's wrong with that?"

Putnam didn't answer. He just paddled away. He had to collect his thoughts. At some point he had found himself trusting her, even helping her. But now here she was claiming that she had not only cavorted with coots and vultures and ravens, but that she had also willingly and purposefully approached a mortal enemy, a raptor, a known grebe-killer, a *hawk* for crying out loud! Well, it was too much for him to swallow. Like the ravens, she was just too clever.

He turned and paddled back toward her. "Did you perch?" he asked, hoping to trip her up.

"I can't *perch!*" she said with a laugh. "Grebes don't *perch!*"

*If, in fact, you are a grebe,* Putnam thought. "I thought maybe *least* grebes did," he said slyly. "So how did you ask your question?"

"I circled."

"And what did the hawk do as you circled?"

"She said 'Good day, least grebe.' Hawks know everything."

"Oh?"

"It comes from flying so high above the world,"

Pennyroyal explained. "They can see everything that happens below. They have exceptional eyesight, you know. If you ever need to know anything, ask a hawk, I always say."

"Did she answer your question?"

"Yes. I asked her if there was a place nearby where I could dive, and she said that there was a very deep spring hidden beneath the rushes. Then she led me to it."

"She *led* you?"

"Well, she said, 'Come, I'll show you,' and then flew out over the cienega. She circled over a certain section of it that looked like all the other sections to me, but she said the spring was down there, hidden by the grass."

"That was kind of her," Putnam said, smirking a little.

"Wasn't it?" Pennyroyal said brightly. "But I told her I needed water to land on and she said 'Of course,' and led me to a clearing with a small spring of water that she said wasn't deep but would do for landing. She said I'd have to make my way through the rushes, which she warned me were dense."

*Don't I know it,* Putnam thought.

"She said she would watch over me from above, though, in case I got off course. I was so lucky I met her!"

It occurred to Putnam that, if in fact the hawk had really spoken to Pennyroyal, she'd probably had motives that weren't so awfully kind. Maybe she intended on dropping upon Pennyroyal once she had become mired in the rushes. *Pennyroyal is too trusting,* Putnam thought — and then he felt confused. Was she cunning or naive?

"The landing was rough," Pennyroyal went on.

"You know how it is with us. We can't exactly land on a dime."

Putnam didn't know how it was. He had only landed the one time, and on his bill.

"I skidded off the water into the rushes," she said with a giggle.

Putnam wrinkled his brow. *She thinks it's funny!*

"I guess it was about that time that a beautiful blackbird appeared and asked me if I was all right."

"Red-winged?" Putnam asked.

"Yes. He was so handsome. Like a raven."

*Handsome like a raven?*

"He had such a powerful voice."

"They're very common around here," Putnam said wearily.

"Are they?" Pennyroyal said. "How lucky for you." Then she squinted at Putnam, as if sensing something behind his words. "Don't you like them?"

"No, of course I do," Putnam said, squirming a bit.

Pennyroyal kept squinting at him. He gulped and added, "And d-did he help you?"

"Yes," Pennyroyal said, still eyeing Putnam closely. "He followed along with me, hopping from stalk to stalk. But how he really helped was by keeping me company. It was not much fun out there — the grasses just went on and on — and he told me stories to take my mind off it. He said that, for some reason, pied-billed grebes were always crashing into the rushes. He said once he helped one that had managed somehow to get stuck in the rushes bill-first! Ha! Can you picture it? Then, after all the blackbird had done for it, the grebe just went off without a word of thanks. Can you beat that?"

Putnam sank an inch in the water.

"He said I looked different from the others somehow, and I told him that I was a least grebe, but that I liked to be called a water witch, and that I was a long way from home and he asked me to tell him all about it — where I was from, where I'd been. We talked and talked and talked and then all of a sudden there was the spring!"

*Just like that,* Putnam thought, raising his eyebrows.

"What?" Cora Lee snapped. "Eyebrows? Grebes have eyebrows?"

Well, I said.

"Birds don't have *hair*!" Cora Lee said.

Well, I said again. "They have a kind of, uh, a kind of a . . . a *ridge* — that's it — a ridge of feathers, just over their eyes —

"Pshaw!" Cora Lee said, just like my mother.

Okay, okay, I said. So he didn't raise his eyebrows. He rolled his eyes. How's that?

"Okay," she said. "Now go on, but remember: I'm listening. No more tricks."

I apologized and went on:


"The spring was covered over with a canopy of rushes," Pennyroyal said, "just like the hawk had said. I looked up and saw her circling above. 'Thank you!' I called out. She just dipped her wing a bit and sailed off. I thanked the blackbird, too, and he said he'd leave me to my diving. And then you know what he said? He said, 'I wish sometimes I were a grebe.' Isn't that funny? I mean, here was this beautiful, charming bird —

he was charismatic, is what he was, charismatic. You know?"

Putnam nodded though he didn't know the word.

"And he wished he could be a grebe! I couldn't believe that. Why would he want to be a grebe of all things? Why would anybody *want* to be a grebe?" Her smile faded and she looked down at the water.

Putnam looked down, too. He didn't know what to say. He could think of a lot of things he liked about being a grebe. But he wasn't sure she had really asked him.

"You don't like being a grebe?" he asked at last.

"I'd rather be a hawk. Or an eagle. Or a raven, even. I could name a hundred birds I'd rather be. Like a bufflehead or a pygmy owl or a killdeer. Or maybe a hummingbird, or a swift, or a swallow, or a —"

"Ahem," Cora Lee coughed. She tapped her foot impatiently.

"Shoot, it'd be better to be a groove-billed ani than a grebe," Pennyroyal finished.

I flashed a sly smile at my niece. She rolled her eyes.

Putnam pondered this awhile. It had never occurred to him to imagine himself as some other kind of bird. Truth be told, he had never met a bird that he thought had things any better than he did. Sure, hawks and vultures could soar, hummingbirds could hover, herons could wade, ravens could cluck their tongues, but none of them — none of them — could dive like a grebe.

*Flying was fine,* Putnam thought, *and birds were probably born with wings to do it, but which birds could both fly AND dive? Not ravens, not hawks, not vultures, and certainly not coots! Coots were lousy flyers AND lousy divers!* He almost said, "Well, it could be worse; you could be a coot," but then he remembered how Pennyroyal had said that she'd liked the coots — which he still couldn't fathom — and held his tongue.

"Is that why you left home?" he asked, and then wondered why he did.

Pennyroyal seemed troubled by the question.

She turned her head away and combed the feathers on her back with her bill.

"I'm sorry," Putnam said. "I didn't mean anything. I don't know why I said that."

"It's all right," Pennyroyal said softly, still preening her feathers. "I suppose I did just get a little tired of pond life."

The two sat in silence a moment. Putnam looked around the cave and saw the black eyes of the other grebes looking on in the darkness. He thought about how none of them ever spoke — to each other, to him, how he never spoke to them. And he wondered about grebes, always diving, always hiding, always eating their feathers. And then he looked back at Pennyroyal — Pennyroyal Grebe — and he thought, *What kind of grebe am I?*

"Frank," Cora Lee said, looking at me with an almost parental air. She held her shoulders back and pulled her chin in. "Why did you move away from Terre Haute?"

Terre Haute? I said, a little befuddled. (Terre Haute, Indiana, is where my sister and her husband and Cora Lee live, and also where my mother lives, and where I used to live.)

"You're always flying away," she said patronizingly. "You're always hiding. And you eat your feathers."

My feathers?

"Your nails."

Okay, now, just hold on, I said. I told you this is just a story. Don't go hunting for lessons in it.

"Mom says you left because you're restless," Cora Lee said. "Dad says it's because you're irresponsible."

Does Howard still shoot birds?

Cora Lee smiled. She knew what I meant by that. She's clever all right. (But not *too* clever.)

"Why didn't you come home for Christmas?" she asked.

I don't think one should fly north for the winter, I said.

"Mom says that if you don't come next year I can't visit you for New Year's anymore."

I have a bottle of champagne in the icebox for tonight, I said. Nonalcoholic, naturally.

"I'm serious, Frank," she said. "She means it."

Listen, do you want to hear the rest of this or not? I said. Do you even remember where we were?

She giggled. "Yeah. Penny's at the spring."

That's Penny*royal,* I said.

"Ex-*cuse* me," Cora Lee said. "Penny-*royal*'s at the spring."

\*       \*       \*

"I dove into the water," Pennyroyal went on. "It was very dark, and very deep."

Putnam nodded. This was the part of Pennyroyal's story he was waiting for. "And then what?" he said.

"I dove deeper and deeper," she said. "Deeper than I've ever gone before. There were these pretty glints of sunlight following me down, I remember. They danced in the darkness."

"Yes, yes," Putnam said impatiently. "And *then?*"

"Well, I guess that was when I saw the eye," Pennyroyal said. Her voice lowered. "At least it looked like an eye. It was very black. And big. As I got closer to it, I began to feel something pulling me."

"And then what happened?" Putnam said so urgently that Pennyroyal jumped.

"I dove toward it," she said. "I dove into it."

"You dove *into* it?" Putnam said, shocked.

"Yes, I dove right into it," Pennyroyal said. Her expression fell. "I ended up here." She looked around. "Just like the rest of you."

Putnam looked into her golden eyes. *You're not like the rest of us,* he thought.

Slowly, Pennyroyal began to grow stronger. She still disliked the taste of the mosquito fish — in fact, to her, the taste of them seemed to get worse the more she ate — but she held her breath and imagined that they were caddis nymphs and they seemed to go down a little easier.

Putnam continued his training. He soon was staying under to the count of two hundred. He felt strong and capable. *It's time,* he thought, *to begin Pennyroyal's training.*

"I've been all over this pool," Pennyroyal told him. "There's no way out. And there's no bottom. We're stuck."

"Everything has to have a bottom," Putnam said. "And if there's a way in, there's a way out." He smiled at her.

"I don't know," Pennyroyal said. "I've dived down pretty deep."

"I've dived deeper," Putnam said. "And I'll dive

deeper still. Every time I add a few seconds. I figure I've made it down two hundred feet."

"Impossible!" Pennyroyal said. "Loons are the only birds that can dive that deep!"

"And peng —" Cora Lee started to say.

Pennyroyal had never heard of penguins, I interrupted. Putnam had heard of loons, however — from the coots — but he wasn't aware they dove so well. He wondered if they could really dive deeper than grebes.

"I'll find the bottom," he said. "And I'll find the way out. And if you want to go with me, you'd better start training, too."

Pennyroyal's eyes sparkled a little, just enough to light up her face. "I want to go," she said.

Putnam was humbled to find that Pennyroyal was as fine a diver as he was. Maybe better. She turned crisp, sharp figure eights and dove straight and swift. Her only shortcoming was her endurance. She needed to strengthen her lungs if she was going to be able to dive as deep as he could.

"One hundred and ten!" she gasped as she came up. "I can't believe how deep it is!"

"One hundred," Putnam corrected. "And it's deeper still."

"What if there is no bottom?" Pennyroyal asked, panting.

"There is," Putnam said.

"Where will you go if we find the way out?"

"*When* we find it," Putnam said, "where will *you* go?"

"I don't know," Pennyroyal said, eating a mouth-

ful of feathers. "I don't really have a home anymore. I can't seem to stay in one place for long. Maybe I should, I don't know. But I can't help myself. I get so curious. There are so many places."

*To leave*, Putnam thought.

"Come on," Pennyroyal said. "Let's go down again."

They dove side by side, almost touching, counting to themselves, pushing themselves further downward. Though the water was dark, the golden glow that always danced in it gave them enough light to see one another's outline.

The trick was knowing when to turn back. They couldn't run out of breath at their furthest depth. They needed air to get back up. So they each had to know their own halfway point. Once they reached it, they would quit and turn back. Pennyroyal always had to turn back first. The signal was a tap on Putnam's shoulder with her tiny wing. Then, at the surface, there was always a lot of coughing and wheezing.

"Two thirty-five," Pennyroyal would say, huffing and puffing, and Putnam would answer, "Two ninety-nine." (Pennyroyal tended to count a little fast.)

At some point during their training, they began hearing coughing and wheezing coming from the cave's nooks and crannies and cubbies. They couldn't tell if it was the other grebes or just their own echoes.

And then, after weeks and weeks of training, just as Pennyroyal had reached four minutes (two hundred and twenty seconds to Putnam), their bills hit solid stone.

No pond is bottomless, you know.

Cora Lee nodded. "That's right," she said. "Everett at school told me that Riddle Lake was bottomless. But it's not. I brought up a handful of mud to prove it." She smiled.

That's because you're a water witch, I said, and smiled back at her.

She wiggled her feet.

For a few frantic moments, Putnam and Pennyroyal searched madly for an opening. They were well past their halfway point and knew it; still, their excitement kept them down, hunting, pecking, scouring the bottom for the eye, for a way out. They found none. Finally they simply had to turn back. They swam up toward the surface as swiftly as they could. They could both feel their lungs burning for air. At last, they broke free of the water, wheezing and panting and gasping for breath.

When finally she could speak again, Pennyroyal said to Putnam, "You were right. There is a bottom. Not that it does us any good."

"There has to be a way out," Putnam said.

"It's a stone crypt!" Pennyroyal shouted. "It's sealed up and no one's ever getting out!"

"Then how did we get in?" Putnam said, irritated. "I wasn't *born* here you know!"

"You *weren't*?" Pennyroyal said mockingly. "I would've sworn you were!"

Putnam felt a flush of anger. "No! I wasn't!" he snapped, and then dove, bill-first, under the water.

"Oh, for heaven's sake!" Pennyroyal called after him. "I was only teasing!"

But Putnam couldn't hear her. He was swimming in figure eights as fast as he could. The cold water did not cool his anger.

*I'll get out of here,* he said to himself. *I'll show her. Then let's hear her scoff!*

He swam to the wall of the pool and, following along it, made a lap. The pool was like a huge bowl filled with water, like a pond, only without the sky, without life — just cold stone and cold water and dreary grebes and bitter fish. He dove deeper and swam the perimeter again, and then deeper and deeper, spiraling down along the pool's sides, down toward the bottom. He ignored his turn-back point. His chest began to ache. His head grew dizzy. Pressure built behind his eyes. He had no idea how long he'd been down. He hadn't been counting. If he didn't resurface soon his bill would burst open and his lungs would fill with water. Then he'd *sink* to the bottom.

*Where there's a way in, there's a way out, where there's a way in, there's a way out.* His mind pounded with the thought. *Where there's a way in, there's a way out, where there's a way in, there's a way out.* Round and round he swam, down and down, searching where he'd searched a hundred times before, searching in vain.

Finally, unable to stay closed a second more, his bill opened and the dark, cold water rushed in. He sank like a stone.

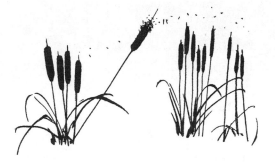

*He awoke on the ledge.*

"I don't know your name," a voice said to him from above. "What do I call you?"

His eyes focused and he saw Pennyroyal sitting beside him, looking down into his eyes. Her face looked worried.

"We pumped a lot of water out of you," she said.

Putnam looked up at her, perplexed.

"Yes, *we*," Pennyroyal said, and waved her wing to indicate the grebes sitting on the water around them. They all nodded. "They brought you up," Pennyroyal said. The grebes nodded again. "Apparently, they've been practicing their diving."

"Two hundred!" called out one of the grebes.

"Two ten!" kucked another, followed by a chorus of numbers.

Pennyroyal smiled at them.

"Putnam," Putnam said to her. "My name is Putnam. Putnam Grebe."

"Putnam?" Pennyroyal said with a laugh.

"Putnam!" a grebe repeated. "Putnam!" said another. "Putnam!" "Putnam!" "Putnam!" Each of them called it out at least once.

Tears gathered in Putnam's eyes. He didn't understand. *Why are they mocking me?* he thought. *What did I say?*

"Putnam is what *all* grebe chicks are called!" Pennyroyal said. And another round of "Putnams" arose from the grebes. "I was a Putnam once my-self!"

Putnam suddenly heard his mama calling the brood: "Mm-put-put-put."

He suddenly felt very empty, as if a lot of what he was had just been taken from him. He looked at Pennyroyal's smiling face and couldn't make up his mind who she was, what was true, whether he wanted to run and hide or stay and thank her. He couldn't make sense of anything. He didn't know what was what anymore. He didn't know which way was up.

"When I left home," Pennyroyal said, "I gave myself the name Pennyroyal. I was alone on my new pond. There was no one to name me."

"No one to name me," the cavern echoed.

The grebes sank into the water up to their chins.

"I was looking for the way out," Putnam said.

"I figured," Pennyroyal said, patting his back with her tiny wing. "There isn't one. We'll just have to stay here and make the best of it."

"But don't you want to leave?" Putnam asked. "You like leaving."

Pennyroyal twisted her long neck around and dug some down out from under her wings. She swallowed it, then said, "I think I'll try staying."

"You want to stay *here?*" Putnam asked.

"Well, it wouldn't be my first choice. But I don't really see that I have *any* choice."

"There's a way out," Putnam said. "You'll have a choice when we find it."

"Where will you go if we do?" Pennyroyal asked.

"Back to the pond," Putnam said. "The one with the cottonwoods and the willows and the ravens and the turkey vultures. The one with the coots."

"Oh!" Pennyroyal gasped. "That was *you?*"

Putnam didn't need to answer.

"And the red-winged blackbird? It was *you* that got stuck in the rushes, bill-first?"

*She is clever,* Putnam thought.

"But how can that be?" Pennyroyal said. "You're so able and confident. You're so helpful! You're just about the finest grebe I've ever met!"

"Ever met!" the cave echoed.

Putnam wanted to say, "No! *You* are the finest grebe *I've* ever met!" but he worried that it might not seem genuine. Unoriginal. Like an echo. So instead he said, "No, I'm not."

"When we get out," Pennyroyal said, "let's head back to the pond. I'll give bloodworms another try."

Putnam laughed. "There aren't any left!" he said. He shook his head. "Stupid coots!"

In time, spring came to the world above. By then all the grebes had trained hard enough to be able to reach the pool's bottom. They had also grown to almost enjoy the taste of the mosquito fish. They no longer went out of their way to avoid one another. In fact, they played together. They made up pool games, much like children do. They played a grebe version of water tag, and a grebe version of Marco Polo. They held races to see who was the fastest, and diving contests to see who could stay under the longest. It was during just such a game, in fact, that, deep beneath the surface, Putnam and Pennyroyal found the golden eye.

They had been chasing one another around the pool, one trying to touch the other with his or her bill, then switching roles, the hunter becoming the hunted, and vice versa.

"Tag!" Cora Lee squealed and wiggled her feet.

Right. And then, as they were whirling around and around and laughing silently underwater, a golden light in the shape of an eye — a grebe's eye, that is; a circle — opened and lit up the pool. Putnam looked at Pennyroyal beside him, flooded in golden light. Her golden eyes looked white. Then suddenly, he felt a push. It was strong, like a current, and felt much like the pull that had dragged him from the cienega — only in reverse. It pushed him *away* from the golden eye.

"But the other eye was *black*!" Cora Lee said.

That was going in, I said.

"Hmm," she said with a nod. "I get it. The cave was underground so the eye was black. The spring had sunlight in it, so the eye was gold."

Sounds reasonable, I said.

An instant later, a grebe shot past Putnam, followed by a small school of mosquito fish.

"Pennyroyal?" Cora Lee asked herself.

When Putnam surfaced a few moments later, coughing and wheezing and gasping for breath, he clambered up onto the ledge and flopped down on his side. Then he passed out.

When he awoke, the grebes were all gathered on the water before him.

"Where is she?" one asked.

"We can't find her," another kucked.

Putnam lifted his head and looked out over them. "She's gone?"

The grebes all nodded. All except one, that is. She was off to the side, away from the others, looking nervous and confused.

*The new one,* Putnam thought. *From the eye.*

*"Poor Putnam," Cora Lee said sadly.*

Poor *Putnam*? I said. I thought you didn't like him.

"I know. But I feel sorry for him."

But he got what he wanted. Pennyroyal was gone.

"That's *not* what he wanted," Cora Lee said smugly.

What did he want?

Cora Lee rolled her eyes at me. "You don't know? You *know*. It's *your* story. You tell me!"

Well, it's almost over. Why don't I just finish.

"Suit yourself," Cora Lee said with a shrug.

\*　　\*　　\*

Life under the cienega returned to its former routine. The grebes stopped their diving and their playing and resumed their shadowy ways, lurking in dark caves and disappearing into the black water whenever they caught sight of one another. The new grebe followed suit. She fit right in.

Putnam often caught himself doubting whether Pennyroyal had ever been there at all. He sometimes wondered if he hadn't dreamt her. But in his heart he knew she'd been there. He knew she had come and gone through the golden eye. He knew she was at the pond, eating caddis nymphs and cavorting with the coots as the sun sank behind the cottonwoods and the willows.

Or perhaps, by now, she had already been there and gone.

Putnam gave a lot of thought as to why he gave in to the push — why he didn't just dive into it and through the eye, as Pennyroyal did. He'd understood what the push was, what it meant. He knew that he had to swim into it if he wanted out. The first time, on the way in, he hadn't cared where he was or where he went. He'd felt helpless and hapless and lost. So he didn't resist. He let the pull take him where it wished. But this time, he had cared where he was and where he went. He'd wanted to go.

Or so he thought.

The truth was, when the push came to shove, he'd been afraid — afraid to stand up to it, and afraid to leave. It had suddenly terrified him to think of going back out into the world of coots and hawks — and Pennyroyal Grebe. And so he gave up, he didn't try, and because he didn't, Pennyroyal was gone through the golden eye and he was trapped in the pool — he and the grebes and the golden light.

And now, even if he wanted to, how could he leave? When would the eye open again? Would it open again? How could he predict, how could he know when to be there, deep below the surface, ready to go? And would he be ready to go? Or would he give in again to the push?

*There's only one way to find out,* he thought. *I'll just have to go down there and stay down there as often as possible and for as long as possible and if it ever opens again and the push returns, I'll see if I'm ready. I'll find out if I'm ready to face the coots and the hawks. I'll find out if I'm the grebe Pennyroyal says I am.*

*I hope,* he said to himself, *that when it opens again, that I dive in bill-first.*

*In the meantime, I should think of a name.*

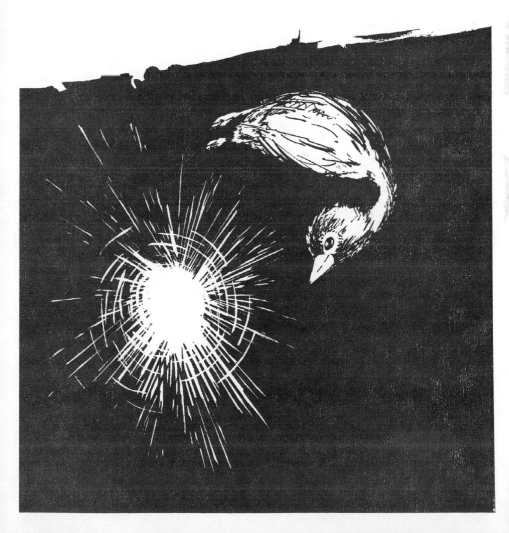

*The end, I said.*

Cora Lee looked up at me. She looked upset.

"*The end?*" she said. "What do you mean, '*The end*'! That can't be *the end!*"

I explained to her that that was the whole story, or as much of it as I'd ever heard.

"But did he get out?" she demanded. "Is he still down there? Come on! That's not the end! If that was the end, how would anybody know the story? How would anybody know he was ever down there in the first place?"

I took off my hat and scratched my noggin. I don't know, I said. Pennyroyal?

"*Pennyroyal!*" Cora Lee shouted. "I thought you

said this was a *true* story! Now you're telling me that a *grebe* started it?"

Well, I said, if a grebe didn't start it then who did? The only ones down there in the cave were the grebes — the grebes and the mosquito fish. Maybe, I said, it was one of the mosquito fish. Maybe one of them escaped with Pennyroyal.

Cora Lee made a face at me — one of those tongue-out, eyes-crossed faces. She must get her manners from her dad's side of the family.

Right about then, the sun started dropping behind the craggy, brown, snow-capped mountains and the temperature fell right along with it. The difference in degrees between day and night in the desert is like, well, night and day.

We better get going, I said.

I started reeling in my line (no cane pole for an old hand like me). We hadn't had even so much as a nibble all day, but I wasn't going to be the one to mention it. My ankle's reputation was at stake.

Cora Lee didn't budge. Her eyes were locked on the tip of her pole.

"So what about Christmas next year?" she asked.

We'll see, Cora Lee, I said.

She shot me a withering look. "Then I guess you won't ever see me again!" she said.

Now, Cora Lee —

"No!" she snapped, holding up her palm. "I won't be able to come here anymore, and you sure won't come to Indiana — *so that's it*! You won't see me anymore *forever*!" And with that she turned her head away.

"I *want* to come," I said to the back of her head. "It's just your dad. Howard and I don't exactly see eye to eye on things. Then your mom gets sore at me for quarreling with him and then your grandma gets sore because everybody's quarreling and it's Christmas and we should all be happy.

I stopped and took a deep breath.

It's just not worth it, I said.

"Maybe *I'm* just not worth it," she said.

Don't be silly, I said. That's not it —

"Mama says you and Dad are just too much

alike," Cora Lee went on. "She says your problem is that you don't want to admit it."

Alike! I said. He's a *hunter*! I'm a —

Before I could finish my sentence, Cora Lee's line suddenly twitched. A fin flapped in the water and she jumped to her feet.

"I got one!" she said.

She gave her line a jerk and up out of the water came a fish, caught on her hook, flopping this way and that. It was a good seven inches long.

"A bullhead!" she squealed, pulling her pole in, hand over hand.

And a good-sized one, too! I said.

I waded out a foot or so and caught the fish in our net. Cora Lee unhooked it like a pro (she doesn't have a squeamish bone in her body) and dropped it into the fish bucket.

I guess the coots didn't scare them away after all, I said.

"We can have it tonight," she said. "It'll be our last fish fry together."

Now, don't be silly, Cora Lee, I said. We'll fry

plenty more fish together. Why, next year I bet we snag every exotic in the pond!

Cora Lee looked up at me, slowly shaking her head from side to side. "Not if you don't come for Christmas," she said. "Mama said."

I don't know, I said, looking away from her, out at the pond. The sunset had changed the color of the water. The pond was now one big, golden circle. I want to come, I said again. If only it weren't for Howard.

Cora Lee smiled a knowing smile. "Come on, Frank," she said, nudging me with her elbow. "Don't be a Putnam."

I laughed. Such a clever girl. Perhaps a *little* too clever.

Okay, *Cora*, I said, leaving off the Lee. Anyone as clever as she is ought to be able to be called what she likes. I'll fly north next winter.

Her feet wiggled. "I'll hang your stocking over the fireplace," she said.

We packed up our things and started making our way back to the truck. As we walked along the pond, I noticed that Cora Lee kept peering into the rushes pretty intently. Every now and again she'd stop and crouch down and look real hard into a clump or a clearing, then she'd just shake her head and run to catch up with me.

Lose something? I'd ask each time.

"Just thought I saw something," she'd always answer. Then we'd keep on our way.

Then one of those times, as she was bent over, looking into the grass, she started jumping up and down and waving at me to come on over and whispering as loud as she could, "*There they are! It's them!*" By the time I got there, "they" apparently had disappeared. All I saw were circles in the water that told me something had been there and gone. A few bubbles on the surface confirmed this.

"*It was them!*" Cora Lee said. "*It was Putnam and Pennyroyal!*"

I squinted at her. How do you know? I asked. Did you see their toes?

"Yes!" Cora Lee hissed.

Were they lobed?

"Yes!"

Maybe they were coots.

"No!" she said. "They weren't black! They were *brown!*"

How did they go under? I asked.

"Bill-first! But they came up submarines!"

Did their heads look like baby box turtles?

"YES!" Cora Lee yelled, hopping a little.

Did they eat their own feathers?

"Frank!" She scowled at me. "I didn't see them *that* long!"

Well, I said, scratching the stubble on my jaw. What color were their eyes?

Cora Lee simmered down a bit at that one. I could see she was mulling it over. Then a smile spread across her face and, at last, she said, somewhat coyly, "Why, black and gold, of course." She flashed me a three-dollar smile. And some change.

Well, then, I said, it was probably them.

"It was *definitely* them!" Cora Lee said, pretending to be outraged. "You think I was telling you a fish story?"

Naw, I said. I reckon you just finished my grebe story.

"Chonk, chonk, bweep-bweep, BWAAK!" a coot out in the middle of the pond replied.

Just like a coot to try and get the last word.

# About the Author

*Patrick Jennings* grew up in Crown Point, Indiana, and central Arizona. After graduating from Arizona State University, he relocated to San Francisco, where he taught English as a Second Language. That experience led him to move to San Cristóbal de las Casas, Chipas, Mexico, where he set his first novel for young people, *Faith and the Electric Dogs*. A 1996 *Booklist* Editors' Choice, *Faith and the Electric Dogs* was hailed by critics as "imaginative and full of fun" (*School Library Journal*) and as "a captivating tale narrated with brio" (*Publishers Weekly*, starred review). It was followed by a sequel, *Faith and the Rocket Cat*, which *Kirkus Reviews* called "as refreshingly unconventional as the original . . . a blissful multilingual escapade." Patrick Jennings lives in Arizona with his wife, Alison, and their baby daughter, Odette.